Somebody ♡ Somewhere

In Texas

A Novel

Connie Lewis Leonard

Victoria,
Remember
God loves
you always and
forever. You are
especially Blessed
Somebody Somewhere
in Texas loves
You.
Connie Lewis Leonard

Garcon Publishing

Somebody Somewhere in Texas

Published by Garcon Publishing Company

Copyright 2016, by Connie Lewis Leonard

ISBN-13:978-1539015550
ISBN-10:1539015556

Scriptures are taken from the Holy Bible:
THE HOLY BIBLE, NEW INTERNATIONAL VERSION®, NIV® Copyright © 1973, 1978, 1984, 2011 by Biblica®. Used with permission.

Cover photo Copyright 2016, by Charles Gregory Reeves. Photographs may not be reproduced without express written permission from the photographer: charlesreaves1@aol.com

Cover design Copyright 2016, by Jackie Castle, at Jackie Castle's Story World.

This book is dedicated to my Lord and Savior, Jesus Christ, for giving me life, love, health, and opportunity.

Heartfelt appreciation goes to my husband, family, and friends who have encouraged and supported me through life and my writing journey.

I am thankful for the many learning opportunities through American Christian Fiction Writers, the DFW/ACFW Ready Writers, North Texas Christian Writers, ClassSeminars, and Jerry Jenkins Christian Writers Guild. A special thanks to Granbury Writers' Bloc as we have learned and developed our writing skills together.

I am grateful for special friends who critiqued this novel, catching errors and offering feedback: Lorna Cockerham, Peggy Purser Freeman, Lyn Goodgion, Marilyn Hayworth, Linda Manning, and Connie Newsom.

"Brothers and sisters, I do not consider myself yet to have taken hold of it. But one thing I do: Forgetting what is behind and straining toward what is ahead"

Philippians 3:13

New International Version

Chapter One

"The Yellow Rose of Texas" ringtone shattered the silence in the efficiency kitchen. Katie's pulse raced two beats faster than the song. How long had it been since he'd called? As she picked up the cell phone, the pulsating vibration jarred her entire body. "Hel— hello."

"Katie, this is Dad."

Hearing his voice after all those years made her heart do a belly flop.

"Katie, are you there?"

She swallowed hard, closed her eyes, and pictured his brown eyes buried beneath bronzed, weather-beaten skin. Old before his time, working in the wind and rain, the blistering heat, the frigid cold, trying to make a living on the small family ranch. She inhaled. "Yes, Dad, I'm here."

5

A prolonged pause before she heard his voice. "I know it's been a long time since we talked—too long."

"Six years." She leaned her head on the doorframe, trying to keep the pain and anger out of her voice.

"That's what happens when two people are so stubborn."

"Two people? *Which* two people, Dad?"

"You and your mother."

She shook her head and paced between the kitchen and living area of the small apartment. "And what about you, Dad?"

"You know me, I've always tried to keep the peace with your mother and leave the raising to her."

Opening the refrigerator, she hoped the cold air would neutralize the heat sizzling in her head. She pulled out a mineral water and took a long sip. "How much peace have *you* had the past six years?"

"Not much," he said quietly. He took in another deep breath. "I've missed you terrible bad. LeAnn kept me up with what was going on, told us about the boy."

The pent-up emotion spewed over the dam. "You mean the illegitimate child that tarnished your status as a deacon and Mom's position as president of the Women's Missionary Association? The child I bore alone and have cared for with no help from anyone but Aunt LeAnn?"

He sobbed. She'd never heard her dad cry. "Katie, I'm sorry. I sent you cards and money when I could, but I was afraid to call, afraid this would happen."

"Thanks for the money. Thanks for signing the cards with your name but nothing else, not even 'I Love You.'" The words sounded cruel, but she couldn't hold back, not once the flood began. "Yeah, I guess I should have sent you a great big Thank You note signed with hugs and kisses."

He sobbed again. "I loved you from the day you were born, even before you were born, but I'm not good with words."

The tears flowed from her broken heart. "I could never please Mom. Growing up I wondered what was wrong with me. When I was a teenager, I realized she resented me because her pregnancy *with me* ruined her plans. Then when I got pregnant that threatened to ruin her respectability, her prestige in the church, her reason to live." She wiped the tears and blew her nose. Gasping for breath, she said, "Yeah, I thought *you* loved me until the day you stood there and let Mom tell me what a disgrace I was, tell me she never wanted to see me again, and you did nothing." Sobs shook her socks off.

"I'm sorry, Katie." His ragged, irregular breathing scared her. She didn't want him to have a heart attack or stroke on the phone. "When you left, you took my sunshine away."

What a sucker punch! He never told her he loved her, but he had sung lullabies and love songs in his smooth baritone voice. "You Are My Sunshine" was her favorite. She believed she was until she turned up pregnant at nineteen. "Yeah, well, I haven't exactly been walking in sunshine the past six years, either."

"No, but you had a chance to follow your dream. LeAnn gave you something I couldn't."

She paused, trying to regain her composure. "So why are you calling now, after all this time?" *Did she really want to know?*

"Your mother has cancer." He took a few more erratic breaths. "She wants to see you. She wants to try to make things right. She wants to see the boy, too." More fitful breaths. "Please come home. *I need you.*"

She imagined her strong-willed mother fighting a foe bigger and more powerful than her, her strong, dependable dad needing her, and she closed her eyes at the distressing image.

"Katie," deep breaths, trying to regain his manly demeanor, "Doc says it's pretty serious. The cancer spread before they found it."

She paused, trying to calm the pounding in her head as her pulse played leap frog. Her weak knees forced her to sit. "Aunt LeAnn probably told you I'm teaching. There are two more weeks of school. Can it wait that long?"

"Yes, she told me, and I'm real proud of you. I'll wire you the money tomorrow, and you come as soon as you can, K?"

"I'll let you know when I make arrangements."

"Thanks." He took a deep breath and said softly, "I do love you with every beat of my heart." The phone clicked.

She tiptoed into Austin's room and kissed him. His long, dark lashes fluttered against his creamy cheeks. *All things work together for good. Even from my sin came something beautiful. But if I go home, everyone will know.*

***

Richard Kane met them at the Lubbock Airport. He hugged his daughter tight until she coughed for air. "Katie, you're still the most beautiful girl in the world." He ruffled Austin's thick, wavy hair. Bending down, looking him full in the face, he said, "Hi, I'm your grandpa. It's nice to meet you."

The little gentleman extended his hand. "It's nice to meet you, Sir."

Richard stood. "You've done a good job, Katie. He's real mannerly." As they walked toward the luggage carrousel, he spoke barely above a whisper. "He has the deepest blue eyes I ever saw . . . almost. Really stands out with that black hair."

She shook her head. She didn't want to discuss it. Didn't want her dad to mention it. She dreaded her mom's comments when she saw Austin. Yes, she could have tried to make amends, but she hadn't wanted to come home for this very reason.

They drove two hours to the ranch. Two hours through flat West Texas in his old pickup. Her dad talked excitedly, telling Austin about his cattle and horses, the four-wheeler, his prize bull.

She had kept up with the weather, stocks and commodities. She knew that another year or two of drought and all the small, independent ranchers in Texas would be out of business, her dad included. Five generations of The Kane Ranch blown away by the West Texas wind. Dry and barren just like her heart.

Chapter Two

They turned off the county road onto Kane Lane, surrounded on both sides by pasture, cattle grazing on the east side, coastal bermuda growing on the west. Large trees shaded the house, a cool oasis in the flat, dry land. Duke and Daisy greeted them with excited barks, doing a salsa dance with the wheels of the pickup. When Katie opened the door of the truck, Duke jumped into her lap, whining and licking her in the face. Throwing her arms around him she said, "I've missed you, too, Old Boy."

Daisy jumped up, shoving Duke onto Austin's lap. His eyes grew large as the blue heeler sniffed and licked his face. Living in Chicago, Austin had never been around dogs, except a few little neighboring fluff balls. "Down, Duke, Daisy." Dad snapped his fingers and the dogs instantly obeyed, jumping out of the pickup.

"These are Grandpa's cow dogs. They won't hurt you." Austin

blinked back tears. She hugged him. "It's okay. They'll be your best friends once they get to know you."

Dad made the dogs sit and showed Austin how to put his hand out to let them sniff. "They get to know people by smell. They probably already know you belong to your mamma, which means you belong to them."

Handing Austin his backpack, they got the rest of the luggage out of the bed of the truck. The swing and wooden rockers swayed in the afternoon breeze on the front porch. Opening the double doors, the living room looked unchanged, a model picture for *Southern Living Magazine*, but instead of the smell of Pine Sol and Lemon Pledge, a dusty, musty smell prevailed. Resounding silence echoed through a house normally filled with music. Katie walked down the short hall to her room, the same lavender comforter covered her bed, the same lacy curtains tied back above the window seat, flooding the room with light. Her bulletin board filled with ribbons and certificates, her megaphone in the corner. She opened the closet, half filled with old clothes, her cheerleading and band uniforms. Leaning her head on the door frame, memories warred with each other—so much happiness and joy, so much disappointment and failure.

Dad cleared his voice. "Um, I thought we'd put the boy in the spare room."

Setting down the bags, Katie took a deep breath before turning. "Austin and I share a bedroom in our apartment. He'd probably be happier sleeping in here with me."

Dad deposited the rest of the bags. "K. I'll go check on your mother while you settle in."

She sat on the bed and pulled Austin into her lap. "This was my room. I was seven when my parents built this house. My mom made the comforter, curtains, and the cushions on the window seat and chair. I'd sit in the window seat and practice my violin for hours. In the evenings, we'd sit on the front porch and your grandpa and I would play together."

"He plays the violin like you and Aunt LeAnn?"

"Yes, we come from a musical family. Someday, if you keep practicing, you'll probably be better than all of us."

His sweet smile lit up his face. "You really think so?"

"I'm sure of it." *Especially if he inherits his dad's talent.*

"Katie, your mom's awake. She'd like to see you."

Saying a silent prayer, she took Austin's hand and led him to her parents' bedroom. She had tried to prepare Austin for her mother's illness, but nothing could have prepared her. Lying in the big, rustic, four-poster bed, her mother looked like a shrunken miniature of the beautiful, vibrant woman who reigned over home and hearth, church socials, weddings, and community get-togethers.

Filled with sympathy and shame, she knelt beside the bed and took her mother's hand. "Hey, Mom." Her voice cracked.

"No tears, Katie. Your homecoming is a joyous occasion,

something I've been praying for." She pulled her daughter's hand to her lips and kissed her fingers. "Your beautiful hands, your talented, musical hands. Kane hands, like your grandmother Kathleen, your namesake."

"Just a different kind of talent than you have. Nobody could hold a candle to your sewing and needle work. And your pies." Closing her eyes, she could smell the cinnamon and spice, taste the flakey, melt-in-your mouth crust. "I've tried but I can't begin to compete."

"Competition is for Four-H and fairs, not families." Mom tried to raise her head. "I want to see the boy."

Wrapping her arm around her son, Katie pulled him forward. "Austin, this is your grandmother."

Mom stroked his soft, angelic cheeks. Smiling she said, "Austin, you are a handsome boy. You have beautiful eyes." Katie lowered her gaze praying her mother wouldn't say anything else. "I guess your mom told you I'm recovering from surgery. I'll be better in a couple weeks, and we can play, maybe bake some cookies. Would you like that?"

"Yes, Ma'am. I 'specially like chocolate chip."

"I have lots of cookie cutters, but we could make a big chocolate chip cookie and decorate it like the ones they have at the mall in Lubbock. That would be fun." He nodded his head.

Dad walked into the room with a covered hospital mug of

ginger ale. He held the flexible straw to Mom's lips and said, "Donna, you rest now. I'll fix us some dinner and bring you some soup and applesauce in a little while." Taking a drink seemed to exhaust her energy, but she smiled and nodded.

Austin and Katie followed Dad into the pristine kitchen, the immaculate white cabinets filled with the same blue and white stoneware they'd used forever. "I marinated some steaks and have fresh corn on the cob to cook. I don't like to cook inside cause I don't want to mess up your mom's kitchen."

"What have you been eating?"

"Your mom's friends have been good to bring food over, mostly soups, something easy for your mom to eat. I cook my breakfast in the iron skillet on the grill. Your mom is real sensitive to smells right now, especially sausage and bacon. I eat a sandwich or something for lunch. In the evenings, if I get hungry for meat, I grill a steak or go to the cafe in town."

Overwhelmed with a deep sense of guilt and grief, Katie hugged him. "I can't cook like Mom, but I can cook. You have enough to do to take care of the ranch."

He held his daughter close, patting her head. "Thanks for coming."

***

Sunday morning, Dad jumped around like a jittery thoroughbred pawing at the starting gate. Katie didn't want to go to church with him. She didn't want to see people from her past. She didn't want them to see Austin, to make comments about his beautiful violet eyes outlined by long, black lashes, his wavy black hair. But Dad begged her to go with him. He said she'd like his new church, a cowboy church, where everyone's welcome and Jesus meets you at the door.

It sure sounded different from the stuffy old First Church, with the catty, critical missionary ladies, the pious, phony deacons, and the pastors who were called and then "called away" through the years. Katie had searched for a church in Chicago, but she didn't find one where she felt comfortable. In spite of some bad experiences in their little, small town church, she still held fast to conservative beliefs. Like believing that the Bible is God's Word, every bit of it as true today as it was two thousand years ago. And like believing Jesus is God's only begotten Son, born of a virgin, crucified on a cross and raised on the third day to save us from our sin, the *only* way, the *only* truth, the *only* life. And as much as she loves classical music, the good old-time gospel hymns held a special place in her heart. Nope, didn't find that in the cosmopolitan city of Chicago.

Dad and Katie took Austin to the Little Wranglers Children's Church. He looked out of place with his khaki pants, polo shirt, and black loafers. Most of the little boys wore faded jeans, cowboy hats, and boots. Dad led her into the sanctuary, which looked more like a barn decorated for a hoe-down, with saddles and a horse trough

16

baptistery. They sat in chairs in the middle of the building. The band began playing. Then she heard his voice. That smooth, mesmerizing voice flowing like the peaceful river he sang about. Paralyzed, Katie wanted to run, but he'd see her. And then he did. The guitar froze, the voice halted, his piercing violet eyes held hers, transfixed, but only for a moment. Then his professional stage presence prevailed, his voice deepened, filled with passionate emotion.

She looked at Dad, but he was staring straight ahead. She shook his knee. "How could you?"

He didn't respond. She started to stand, but he held her back. "Don't go. You've been running too long."

Katie kept her head down as the band played. The preacher walked to the stage when the band walked off. Katie glanced up to see *him* watching her as he walked down the side aisle. Thank goodness there were no empty seats nearby.

The preacher preached—about something. Katie prayed, not for the lost, not for the backslidden, not for the sick, but for strength and speed to get away, away from humiliation and shame. After the closing prayer, she sprang from her seat and hurried toward children's church to rescue Austin before the birds of prey honed in on him.

The band stood at the back exit, shaking hands, being congratulated and thanked for the awesome music. Katie tried to slide past unnoticed, but she had to wait in line with her identification slip. *Really? I can understand extreme security measures in Chicago, but here in West Texas ranching country?*

She squinted through her peripheral vision. Brooks was rubbernecking. *God, if he sees Austin, he'll know. Please don't let him make a scene.*

"Katie Kane, is it really you?" The plump redhead squealed. "You look great!"

"Shelby?" The round head bobbed in affirmation. "I, um, it has been a long time. I almost didn't recognize you." Katie handed her the identification paper.

"Austin," her voice halted, "Kane." Shelby's probing eyes said it all. She gazed down at the boy. Ruffling his black hair she said, "Maybe we can get together for lunch or something?"

Katie put her arm around her son and guided him out the door. Before she reached the exit of the church, Brooks caught her arm. "Katie!"

She pulled Austin closer, shielding him with her body as she hurried out the door. His little legs couldn't keep up with her hurried stride, and he stumbled. Brooks reached to steady him the same time she did. She pushed his hands away. "Don't! Don't touch him!"

Brooks looked wounded, a tempest churning in those deep violet eyes "Katie, why didn't you tell me?"

"It's none of your business." She hurried away but couldn't outdistance the stride of his long, lanky legs. She reached her dad's pickup, but it was locked.

Brooks leaned on the door. "Katie, how can you say it's none of my business? Look at him."

Her body shook like a tornado and tears streamed down like a thunderstorm. Austin pulled away and yelled, "Stranger danger!"

She knelt beside him and put her hand over his mouth. "It's okay. There's no danger."

"Brooks, if you'll excuse us, I need to take my family home now." Dad unlocked the door and helped them inside. Brooks slumped his six-four frame over like someone had punched him in the gut. Katie buried her face in Austin's hair and wept on the silent drive home. After they changed clothes, she sent Austin out to play and confronted her dad in the kitchen.

"Dad, you had no right to put me in that position." He sat at the table with his head bowed. "How long has Brooks been home?"

"About three months. His dad has liver problems—he was a heavy drinker, you know. Brooks has been singing at our church about six weeks."

"You should have told me. It was unfair to put me and Austin in that position."

"Maybe so." He took a long drink of his coffee. "I've missed you something terrible, but you're an adult, and it was your choice. Your mother and I want to get to know our grandson." He rubbed his large, calloused hand over his face. "If I had a son, I'd want to know." He stood and looked out the window. "I don't know what happened between the two of you, but the boy has a right to know his father."

"The *boy* has a right to know that he is loved and wanted by the people in his life." She poured herself a drink of coffee and nearly choked on the bitter brew. "The *boy* has a right to feel safe and secure, to know where he's going to be and who's going to be there with him."

The phone interrupted her tirade. They don't even have Caller ID, for crying out loud. Dad answered on the third ring. "Brooks, I don't think today would be a good time to talk."

Katie grabbed the phone. "I don't want to talk to you today, tomorrow, or ever." She slammed the phone on the receiver, stormed to her room, banged the door shut, and threw herself across the bed. *God, I feel like I'm fifteen. If I could do it all over, I never would have fallen in love with Brooks Travis. But I'd have to go back farther than that—when I was twelve? No, I fell in love with him when I was six years old, riding on the school bus, sitting across the aisle, looking at those eyes, those long luscious lashes, that wavy black hair, that sweet innocent little-boy smile on those full lips. Gorgeous, just like Austin.*

Chapter Three

Brooks shoved his phone in his pocket and stomped into the barn. *Katie hasn't changed a bit. She's still the same little spitfire she was in first grade when she picked up a rock at the bus stop and tried to defend me against a couple of bullies. But now she's not fighting for me—she's fighting against me.*

"What happened, Lord? Yeah, I know. We broke our promise to stay pure until marriage. I loved her so much. I was a selfish kid and was afraid I'd lose her. And then I did. But why didn't she tell me she was pregnant?"

Brooks rubbed his hands along the neck and legs of a muscular blue roan.

"He's a good caballo, strong and fast." His grandfather's voice caught him off guard.

"How's his training, Abuelo?"

"He's learning. He will make a good cutting horse." Roberto Cordova rubbed the horse's nose and whispered in Spanish.

Brooks laughed. "Is he bilingual?"

"Si, your other grandfather speaks to him in English."

"So, it's okay if I ride him."

"Si, work off some of his oats and some of your fury."

"I'm not angry." He didn't mean to snap.

His grandfather raised his bushy eyebrows and curled the end of his handlebar mustache. "A good lather is good for man and beast." He turned and walked away.

Once the horse was saddled, Brooks led him from the corral. When he mounted, the horse snorted and danced around. "Go ahead boy, give me all you got."

Brooks loved the freedom of riding, the wind in his face, the exhilaration of a high-spirited horse. His grandfathers were master horsemen: Abuelo, the horse-whisperer, and Gramps, the strong, disciplined trainer. Together they breed and train the best ranch horses in West Texas. Brooks felt blessed to be raised by his two grandfathers while his father was off riding the rodeo circuit, drinking, and chasing skirts. How did his sweet, godly mother put up with it all these years?

God, I swore I'd never be like my dad, but here I am. I have a son I didn't know about. I hurt the only woman I've ever loved. I never looked at another girl until Katie broke up with me. From what she said, I figured she'd end up with some citified, symphony sissy. Maybe

22

she's married, but that little boy is mine. Even though we only crossed the line one time, there's no mistaking those Castilian Cordova eyes.

Before he knew what he was doing, Brooks found himself at the old oak tree. He dismounted and tied the horse to the fence post. He traced the carved heart with his fingers: "B + K = love." He repeated the childhood rhyme, "Brooks and Katie sitting in a tree. K-i-s-s-i-n-g. First comes love. Then comes marriage. Then comes Katie with a baby carriage."

"We sure did get it backwards, didn't we, God?" He pressed his face against the rough bark. "Please forgive me, Lord." As tears ran down his cheeks, he sobbed, releasing the pent-up emotion and hurt he'd carried far too long. He felt drained when he remounted the horse and headed home. Yes, home. Home from the life of a wandering minstrel, a dreamer. Home from the honky-tonks and bars. Home from the partying and wild women. "Lord, I'm Coming Home."

***

Brooks sat at the kitchen table watching his mother cook supper. She was still a beautiful woman—a good figure, full lips, shiny black hair, long lashes, and those distinctive almond-shaped, violet-blue eyes.

"What are you staring at?" Her smile said so much about her. Never complaining. Never whining. Always thinking of others.

"You're a wonderful woman, Mom."

She lowered her eyes in her humble way. "Ah, you have the

smooth tongue of your father."

"Why did you put up with him all these years?"

"He's my husband, and I love him." She looked at Brooks like he was six years old again and pointed her finger. "He's your father. You will not disrespect him."

"I don't think he deserves my respect."

"He is your father. That is enough for your respect. Besides, he is sick."

"He's sick because of the life he's lived." He hugged his mother. "I came home for you, not him." Brooks left the kitchen. He didn't want to hurt his mother. She'd been hurt enough by his father and by people who clung to old prejudices. Abuelo accepted that treatment without question because he grew up in another generation where ethnic lines were clearly drawn. His mother accepted it, also, but not without pain.

Brooks walked out to the barn. He watched his father feed the chickens. He had regained much of his strength the three months he had been home. If he stayed off the bottle, he might live a few more years, but he'll never be able to rodeo again. He probably won't be able to do much of anything. All those wasted years. *Lord, I don't want to end up like my dad.*

Chapter Four

Monday morning, Dad took Austin out in his Mule to check cattle. As Katie washed the breakfast dishes, the phone rang. She was afraid to answer it, but she didn't want it to disturb her mother. "Kane residence, this is Katie."

"Katie, please don't hang up."

His words sent a bolt of electricity through her, threatening to knock her to her knees. She pulled out a chair and sat at the breakfast nook, closing her eyes and heart to Brooks and his smooth voice.

"Katie, we need to talk. You pick the time and place, and I'll be there."

Her heart thundered in her chest. Her pulse pounded in her temples. Perspiration popped through her pores. Her resolve shattered, swamping her eyes with tears.

"Katie?"

25

"No," She choked and hung up the phone. Turning the ringer off and covering it with a dish towel, she walked to her parents' room.

"Kathleen, what are you doing?"

Keeping her back to her mother, she cleared her voice. "I turned off the ringer so the phone won't bother you."

Mom patted the bed with her frail, thin hand. "Sit."

Katie heaved her shoulders and shook her head. When she started to leave, Mom said, "Please, Katie?"

She swiped her face, but the tears poured faster than she could wipe them away. Mom took her hand. "Katie, I am so sorry for the way I acted when I found out you were pregnant."

"I know I was a huge disappointment to you."

Mom squeezed her hand. "No, let me talk, while I can." Taking a few deep breaths, she continued, "I've made a lot of mistakes in my life."

"Like me."

Mom lifted Katie's hand to her lips and kissed her fingers. "No, honey, you are one of the greatest blessings of my life." She laid their interlaced hands over her heart, and Katie felt the irregular beating. "I wanted you to have the opportunity to follow your dream, to be all God created you to be."

"Unlike you, who had to give up everything for me?"

"Stop interrupting." She closed her eyes. "Your father and I were *so* in love. We were young and made a mistake. You weren't the mistake—you were the blessing, the good that came from our mistake."

"I don't want Austin to grow up thinking he was a mistake who ruined his parents' dreams."

"Sometimes God gives us new dreams. Look at all the heroes of the Bible. God may have led them one direction just to have them turn around and follow a different path. That's what He did for me." She rose up and reached for her mug of water. After taking a few sips, she lay back down. "Because of my stubborn rebellion, I allowed regret to turn to bitterness, robbing me of the joy God had planned for me."

"Mom, I can't deal with this right now."

"Okay." Her hazel eyes focused on her daughter, the light reflecting golden nuggets in a sea of green. "But you're going to have to deal with Brooks. Now that he's seen Austin, you can't hide the fact that he's the father."

Why couldn't Austin have our hazel eyes instead those stunning Castilian, violet-blue eyes like his father, and his grandmother, and his great-grandfather Cordova? Katie nodded, kissed her mom on the cheek, went to her room and sobbed. *God what am I going to do?*

***

Austin talked non-stop when they came in for lunch. "Grandpa let me drive the Mule. And we counted baby cows, I mean calves." He smiled at his grandfather. "And I got to shoot some medicine in their mouth while Grandpa held them." He took a big gulp of milk. "And Duke and Daisy rode on the Mule with us. Then they'd jump down and chase, I mean herd, the cows."

She smiled and patted his head. "I'm glad you had fun, but now you need to calm down and eat."

"After lunch, Grandpa's going to take me to Porter's to get me a cowboy hat and some jeans and boots and spurs so I can ride a horse."

Katie's stomach did a summersault. She gave her dad a firm look. "Maybe we should wait on going to town."

Austin's face changed from sunshine to thunder. Poor little man. He was used to being disappointed living on her small salary in high flying Chicago, wants and desires taking a backseat to necessities.

She forced a smile. "How long's it been since the horses have been ridden?"

"I ride 'em ever' now and again. Sissy and Peanut are old and gentle enough, they should be okay." His jaw set in determination. "The boy needs a hat, a real hat, not a baseball cap, if he's going to be out in this sizzling Texas sun."

"Alright. How about if I ride Sissy while you go to town? Then tomorrow we can ride together."

"Yay!" Austin squealed.

"Dad, would you mind saddling her while I clean up in here?"

Dad ruffled Austin's hair and gave Katie a peck on the head, like she was still his little girl.

As soon as they walked out the door, Katie used the house phone to call Brooks, the number indelibly etched in her heart like everything else about him. Mrs. Travis answered on the third ring.

"Carmela, this is Katie Kane. May I please speak to Brooks?"

"It's been a long time, Katie." Waiting for the response that didn't come, she continued, "He's out working horses with his grandfathers. Let me give you his cell number."

I wonder if she knows yet. Following the cordial good-byes, Katie called Brooks.

"Hey, can you meet me at the tree?"

"When?"

"Dad's saddling Sissy now."

"I'll beat you there." Katie hung up and shook her head. *As if nothing ever happened. As if we're still young lovers racing to our tree to steal a few hugs and kisses. To talk of dreams and far-away places. Of love and marriage and kids. In his eagerness, he always beat me there.*

***

As she rode Sissy, Katie prayed for wisdom and strength. She walked her horse at a leisurely pace. No hurry. It's been six years. It could wait six more years, or forever. But Brooks won't wait.

There he stood, tall and straight like their old oak tree. His horse, a magnificent blue roan, tethered on his side of the fence, while

Brooks invaded her family's property like he had every right in the world. He walked up and took hold of Sissy's reins.

She pulled back on the reins. "I'm not getting down."

"Katie, we can't talk like this."

"I'm staying right where I am."

Brooks moved to the side of the little sorrel mare, still holding the reins. He took off his hat and looked up at her with those beautiful blue eyes. "Why didn't you tell me you were pregnant?"

Deep breath. *God, please don't let me cry.* "I told you I wanted to get married. I'd give up my scholarship if you'd come home."

"I wanted to follow my dream. I wanted you to go with me. Together, your talent and mine, we'd be great. You could have fit in my world, but I'd never fit in Chicago's high society, symphony stuff." He put his hand on her thigh. Feeling like she'd been branded by a hot iron, she moved the stirrup to push him away.

"I would never drag a child around the country so you could sing at honkytonks, bars and rodeos, with groupies fawning all over you." She turned away. *If I look at him, I'll drown in the deep blue ocean of his eyes.*

"I don't have groupies fawning all over me." He reached up and turned her face toward him. "All I ever wanted was you."

She bit her lip to fight back the tears. "Yeah, me and a recording contract, a gold record, fame, fortune, maybe a movie deal."

He put his large hands on her waist and pulled her from the

horse. Wrapping his arms around her, he held her against his chest until the pounding of their hearts synchronized, clobbering her resistance. She tried to pull away, but he held her tight and kissed her. She felt herself melting. When he slid his tongue in her mouth, she bit down. Hard.

He dropped his arms and stepped back. "That hurt."

"Don't think you can just slip back into my life. Everything's changed." She grabbed the saddle horn and put her foot in the stirrup, but he pulled her back into his arms.

"I still love you, Katie. I've always loved you. I'll always love you. That will *never* change."

"We can't go back, Brooks. It's too late."

He took her face in his hands his eyes an impassioned sea of emotion. "I don't want to go back. I want to go forward with you and our son, to be a family."

The reservoir of tears broke. "It's not going to happen. My mother's dying of cancer. When she's gone, I'm going back to Chicago, to my life, with *my* son."

"*Our* son has a right to know his father. And I have a right to know *my* son."

"You have no rights!"

"He is my son. His blue eyes are the same eyes I see in the mirror every day." His hands gripped her shoulders and jiggled her like a sleeping child. "Work with me on this, Katie. If I have to, I'll

31

get a lawyer, but I'd rather it be peaceful."

She shook her head. "How long are you going to be here?"

"As long as it takes." He lifted her chin, staring her down. "I'll give you till Sunday. If I don't get to see the boy by then, I'll call a lawyer first thing Monday morning."

She nodded, pulled away and got on her horse. "I don't know how to tell him."

He held onto the reins. "What have you told him about me?"

"I told him we loved each other very much, but we were young and you weren't ready to settle down." His head descended to his chest and he dropped the reins. She turned Sissy around and called back over her shoulder, "His name's Austin." She leaned forward and gave Sissy her head. For an old horse, she still runs like a racehorse at Ruidoso Downs.

Chapter Five

All week Katie prayed about what to do. She didn't have the money to pay a lawyer, and her parents didn't need another burden on top of her mother's illness and medical expenses. Austin and Dad became best buds. She'd never seen her son so happy—he loved the dogs, the horses, the cattle, and especially his grandfather. He did need a man in his life, but wouldn't it be worse for him not to get to close, too attached, and be crushed when Brooks left him, or when she took him back to Chicago, to her life?

Me and my big dream of playing in the Chicago Symphony Orchestra like Aunt LeAnn. Oh, yes, she was good enough to get a scholarship to the Music Conservatory of the Chicago College of Performing Arts, with Aunt LeAnn's connections. Living with her aunt while balancing a baby, practice, and school, Katie hung on to her scholarship by the skin of her teeth. She was lucky enough to get a teaching position at a private elementary fine arts performing school. The pay's good, not considering the high cost of living in Chicago. The best benefit is that Austin can attend free of charge, and no way would she allow her son to attend public school in Chicago. She'd come back to Texas first, and that's the last thing she wanted to do.

So God, what should I do?

On Wednesday her mother felt well enough to get out of bed. After dinner of homemade chicken pot pie and banana pudding, Mom wanted to sit on the front porch and be serenaded by her two favorite "fiddle" players. They played some old favorites, "Young Love," by Sonny James, "Pretty Woman," by Roy Orbison, and "I Fall to Pieces" by Patsy Cline. Mom asked Katie to play some "classical stuff." She played Pachelbel's Canon, Bach's "Concerto in D minor, and Handel's "Messiah."

Tears streamed down Mom's face. "Kathleen, you are good, so very good. God gave you a great gift. I hope you'll always remember it's from Him and for Him."

"Let me help you to bed, Mom."

Katie covered her mother with the prayer quilt the ladies from church had made for her. Mom took her daughter's hand and asked her to sit on the side of the bed. "What are you going to do about Brooks?"

"I don't know." She started to stand, but Mom squeezed her hand. "Brooks said if I didn't let him see Austin, he'd get a lawyer. I don't know what to tell Austin."

"Tell him the truth. You and Brooks loved each other since you were kids. I don't know what happened, why you didn't tell us the truth."

"I didn't want Brooks to feel trapped. If you knew I was going to have his baby, you and his family would have pressured us to get married. We just weren't ready. We wanted different things."

"Katie, six years ago I said some terrible things to you. I was disappointed that you got pregnant, but what hurt the most was that you said there were several boys, and you weren't sure who the father was." Her voice cracked, so Katie handed her the mug of water. Clearing her throat she continued. "Anyone can make a mistake when they're in love, but thinking that you had gone completely wild just broke my heart. That was too much for me to accept. I felt like a complete failure as a mother, like I'd failed you and God."

"I said some pretty mean things, too. I'm sorry I lied to you, but I thought it would be easier for everyone to handle than the truth."

"I think you thought it would be easier for Brooks. You thought of him first, above yourself, above us, because that's what real love is. Now think about your little boy, even if being around Brooks will be hard for you."

"I don't know what's best for Austin. I don't want him to be hurt."

"I know you love him, and LeAnn loves him, but he deserves to know the rest of his family. You know what they say about it taking a village to raise a child. Brooks and his family will love the boy, just like we do." Her voice grew soft and raspy.

"Good night, Mom." She leaned over and kissed her mother on the cheek. Turning out the light, Katie started to close the door.

"Leave it open. It's good to hear sounds of family. I've had too much of the sounds of silence."

***

Friday morning Katie called Brooks on his cell phone. "Could you come for dinner after church Sunday?"

A pause. "Sure." Another long pause. "You want me to bring anything?"

"No. Austin wants to go to church with Dad, but I'm staying home with Mom." She paced the kitchen and cleared her throat. "Don't talk to Austin, don't look at him, and don't touch him. Wait till you come here. Follow my lead, and I'll introduce you."

"I've always followed your lead." She could hear his deep, ragged breathing. "Katie?"

"This is for Austin, only. There's nothing between us, so don't touch me again, ever. See you Sunday." She hung up before he could say anything else. *God, please give me strength to get through this.*

Chapter Six

There's nothing between us? That's what you think Kathleen
Marie Kane. But I'll play it your way. I'll follow your lead. I'll be the
perfect gentleman. No more vinegar for you, little Miss Katie Bug. I'll
pour on the sugar and charm you right back into my heart. Unless
you're married. But I didn't see a ring on that dainty finger of yours.

Brooks sang "Somebody Somewhere in Texas" as he worked
with a young gelding in the round pen.

Abuelo smiled as he watched his only grandson. Dean Travis
joined his Pardner at the fence. "Roberto, he has your touch with the
horses. Think he'll stay home and work with us?"

"Ah, it depends on a certain little senorita."

"I figured she'd come home since her mom's sick, but she
made her choice six years ago. I'd hate to see my grandson
brokenhearted again." Dean spit out a stream of tobacco. "I'm out of

37

snuff. You need anything from town?"

"Nah, I don't need nothing."

***

Dean Travis returned from town, red faced, his gray eyes smoldering. He marched up to his grandson. "I just came back from the feed store. Bobby Martin said Katie Kane was at that cowboy church with her dad *and* a little black-haired, blue-eyed boy."

"Those old men at the feed store are worse gossips than a bunch of old hens." Brooks looked away from Gramps. "Yeah, I saw her."

"Is the boy yours?"

"Don't worry about it."

Gramps grabbed Brooks by the arm and swung him around. Dean wasn't as tall, but he was strong and sturdy. "I ain't worried, but I want to know if you have a son and what you're going to do about it."

Brooks pulled away. "I'll handle it."

"I've been thinking about going to that cowboy church. I might just try it out tomorrow." Gramps started to walk away and Brooks grasped his arm.

"You haven't gone to church in years. I don't want you to go." Brooks released his grandfather's arm. "Not this week, Gramps."

"When you were a kid, you used to beg me to go to church."

"Yes, and the only time you went was if I was singing or

38

something."

"You singin' tomorrow?"

"Yes, just like I have been for the past six weeks." Brooks took his hat off and wiped the sweat from his brow. "Wait till next week. Please?"

"I guess one more week won't get me any closer to Hell." He patted his grandson on the shoulder. "You better tell your mama before she hears it from someone else."

"Okay. But please don't tell Dad. I sure don't want him showing up ruining everything."

***

Brooks went in early and sat at the kitchen table while his mother prepared supper. She raised her eyebrows. "Where are your manners? You know you don't sit at my table before you clean up, and with your hat on. This isn't the barn."

"I'm sorry, Mama, but I need to talk to you for a minute."

"Stand up."

"Yes, Ma'am." He stood and removed his hat. "Katie's home."

She nodded. "I answered the phone when she called the other day."

"She has a son."

She turned her back to him, turning the meat in the frying pan. "I heard it through the grapevine."

"He's mine, but I didn't know it till I saw him Sunday."

Turning, she looked up at her son, his troubled eyes a reflection of her own distress. "Now that you know, what are you going to do about it?"

"I'm going to meet him tomorrow. I want to be a father to him, more of a father than my dad ever was to me, but it will depend on Katie."

She wiped at the tears pooling her eyes. "Don't let her walk all over you. It's not fun being a doormat."

He stepped forward and hugged his mother. "I'm sorry for the life you've lived."

"I'm not. My children were my life. Your grandfathers were here for you when your father wasn't. Children need a strong man in their life." She pushed him away. "Go now and make yourself presentable for supper."

"Yes, Ma'am. And please don't say anything to Dad, not yet."

She nodded.

Chapter Seven

Katie spent two days trying to decide what to fix for Sunday dinner. She thought about something fancy, something she learned to cook from Aunt LeAnn, something Brooks hadn't eaten before. She considered chicken cordon bleu, basil orange pineapple chicken, Caribbean pasta with shrimp, or beef with mango sauce. Since Mom was sick, the pantry was down to bare bones. Katie didn't want to go to town and face the stares, hear the whispers. Finally, she settled for plain old roast beef with new potatoes and fresh carrots from the garden, and homemade yeast rolls. Her mother made the best yeast rolls in the world. Katie didn't have her touch, but she'd try. Instead of chocolate mousse cheesecake, she settled for cobbler with peaches from the orchard.

***

Sunday morning, Austin strutted in his new jeans, western

shirt, and boots. He wanted to wear his spurs, but his grandfather dissuaded him. "The cowboy church may look like a barn, but it's still the house of God."

"But some of the boys had on spurs last week." Austin batted his long lashes. That little move might melt the hearts of girls and women, but it didn't faze his grandfather.

"Some people like to show off. A real working cowboy knows the purpose and place for spurs." Dad handed him his new Stetson. "You're a real cowboy, like me. We don't wear our spurs in the house or in the church."

Austin's little chest puffed up. He had become his grandfather's shadow. Clearly he wanted to be just like him.

Katie's chest sank. Austin did need a male role model, like her dad—a good, honest, dependable, hard-working man. What would he do when they went back to Chicago?

***

Katie set the table with the good china, the dishes her great-grandfather brought back from World War II. She fried a batch of okra and sliced fresh tomatoes. She put a country gospel CD in the player, went to her room, fluffed her hair, and touched up her make-up. She took off her jeans and put on a short red and white rayon sun dress that complimented her trim figure and legs, legs that Brooks used to say were the shapeliest in the world. She didn't know why it mattered how she looked, but it did. She wanted to look her best even if she didn't care about Brooks.

When she walked in the kitchen, her mother smiled. "You look beautiful. The table looks lovely. And dinner smells heavenly. I'm feeling better every day. Maybe next week I can cook and you can go to church."

"You've cooked enough in your life. It's okay to rest and let someone else wait on you for a change." She hugged her mother and finished putting the food on the table. When she heard her dad's pickup pull in the driveway, her body stiffened.

Her mother patted her arm. "I've been praying. Everything *will* work out."

Austin ran in the door. "Look what I made. It's a creation wheel. You turn it and it shows what God made on each day. Did you know the whole world was made in just seven days?"

Katie knelt and examined the wheel. "Yes, that's what the Bible tells us."

He waved a coloring sheet in front of her. "Look, the red horse is Sissy and the black horse is Peanut."

"You did a great job coloring in the lines." She stood and raised her eyebrows at her father. "Go put your papers in our room, and we'll hang them on the bulletin board after dinner."

Once Austin disappeared down the hall, her father said, "He'll be here." They heard the roar of an engine. "There he is." He walked out the back door and met Brooks in the driveway.

Her mother patted her arm again. "Relax. It will be okay."

Austin came back in the kitchen just as Brooks walked in the door. He looked from Brooks to Katie and back again.

She cleared her throat. "Austin, this is my old friend Brooks. We went to school together. He's going to have dinner with us."

Brooks leaned down and offered Austin his hand. "Glad to meet you, Austin."

Austin tentatively shook the large hand.

"Why don't ya'll go on in the dining room while I fix the glasses? You want sweet tea or water?"

Both men answered at the same time. "Tea."

Austin said, "I think I'll have tea, too."

Katie almost dropped the glass. "I think you'll have milk."

"Milk sounds good to me, too, if you have enough." Brooks looked at her, but she refused to meet his eyes.

"Let's go sit down." Dad led the way.

"Can I help you?" Brooks paused at the door.

Katie shook her head. She filled the glasses and carried them to the dining room on a tray, and made another trip for the rolls.

She sat next to Austin, across from Brooks, and the family held hands as her father offered the blessing.

"This looks real good, Mrs. Kane," Brooks said as he heaped roast and vegetables onto his plate. "After being on the road for so long, there's nothing like good ol' home cooking."

"I'm not feeling up to cooking. Katie fixed dinner." Her mother offered him a weak smile.

"Thank you, Katie."

His eyes unsettled her. His voice unsettled her. *He* unsettled her. She couldn't look at him. "You're welcome."

Her dad carried the conversation. "The music was real good this morning. 'One Day at a Time' is one of my favorites."

"Thank you, sir."

Passing the rolls, her dad said, "How's the horse business?"

When Brooks started talking about the horses, Austin's interest piqued. He asked some questions and Brooks said, "Maybe your mother could bring you over and I could show you how we train them, maybe start teaching you to rope."

"Or maybe your grandpa can take you over one day." Katie forced a smile.

Looking to his grandfather, he pleaded, "Oh, could you, could you?"

Richard Kane looked from his daughter to Brooks, and back again. "I think it'd be good for you to go."

Switching the subject, Katie said, "Everybody ready for dessert? I made peach cobbler."

"Yummy. Can we have ice cream, too?" Austin's blue eyes sparkled.

"Sure." Katie stood and started picking up the plates.

Brooks stood and picked up his plate. "I'll help you."

She put the plates in the sink and turned on the faucet. "I don't need any help. Go back in there."

Standing close, he whispered, "When are you going to tell him?"

She took the cobbler out of the oven. "Maybe we should let him get used to you first."

"People who've seen him are already talking. They know he's mine. Don't you think it would be better to tell him before he hears it from someone else?" He stood too close, invading her space. She walked into the pantry and took the ice cream out of the freezer. She turned to find him standing in the door, filling it with his presence.

"Let's get through dessert, okay?" He stepped back, but she brushed his arm as she passed. She felt the heat radiate through her being and knew she was blushing. She gritted her teeth. "I told you not to touch me again, ever."

He raised his hands in self-defense. "I didn't touch you. You touched me."

"If you want to be near Austin, you have to stay out of my way." She gripped the ice cream carton with both hands. She wished she could dump the ice cream on his head, or on hers. That would cool things off. She handed him a ladle. "Here, you dip up the cobbler and I'll scoop up the ice cream."

"Okay." He handed her the first bowl of cobbler. "I'm sorry.

I'll try to be more careful." He handed her the second bowl. "Austin wants to see the horses. I think he needs to know before he comes to our ranch."

She nodded. "Did you bring your guitar?"

He looked puzzled. "It's in the pickup."

"When we finish dessert, maybe we can go out on the porch. You could play and sing. Maybe we can ease into telling him somehow."

"Would it be easier if I told him?"

She shook her head. "No, it needs to come from me. Just follow my lead."

"Always." Carrying three bowls of cobbler and ice cream, he followed her into the dining room.

***

"Thanks, Katie. The cobbler was delicious. The whole dinner was delicious." Brooks scooted his chair back. "There's a nice breeze today. Why don't we go outside and enjoy the rockers. I have my guitar in the pickup." His eyes were on her, trying to read her mind, her heart, her soul. "Would you like to get your fiddle and we could play together."

"No, you go ahead. I'll just clean up the table, and then I'll join you." She started picking up the dishes.

"I'll help you." Her mother stood up, holding onto the back of her chair.

"No, I can do it. Go on to the porch, if you feel like. I'll be out shortly."

Dad put his arm around Mom. "Donna, you sure you're up to going outside?"

She smiled. "I wouldn't miss it for the world."

Chapter Eight

As Katie put the food away, rinsed the dishes and put them in the dishwasher, she heard Brooks tuning his guitar. Her mind filled with the image of those hands, so strong, so tender. She closed her eyes. *Lord, please help me be strong. It would be so easy to fall for him again, to get my heart broke.*

Katie took her time, prolonging the inevitable. She could stay inside listening to his magical voice, his gifted guitar playing without him seeing how it affected her. He sang some fun songs like "Billy, Billy Bayou" and "Kalijah the Wooden Indian." When he sang "One Day at a Time," she knew it was time to face the music. The pun made her smile. She took a deep breath. *"Yesterday's gone, sweet, Jesus"*— *help me remember that. Can't look back. Regrets are in the past. Gotta hitch my wagon to a star and keep on trucking.*

Dad and Mom each sat in their rockers. Katie brought out fresh glasses of tea. She handed Austin a glass of water and sat next to him in the porch swing. So many times she and Brooks had sat in this swing, under the moonlight, wishing on a star, holding hands, stealing kisses while her parents sat inside watching TV. Brooks flashed her that sunshine in my soul smile of his. "It's a beautiful day today. Nice breeze. No storm clouds in sight." He sang "The Unclouded Day" and then asked, "Any requests?"

Dad reached over and patted Mom's hand. "'Young Love' is our song."

Katie should have given him the name of some cheating song so her parents couldn't request their song. It wasn't just *their* song. Brooks had sung it to her too many times to count. *Well, there's not just one love for everyone. She would find another love someday, in Chicago, and they would have a good life, a cultured life, a quiet life, a safe and secure life.*

After he finished the song, Brooks took a long drink of sweet tea. "Any other requests?" He looked at Katie, but she lowered her eyes.

"Okay. This is an oldie by one of my favorite singers."

With the first chord, she knew what he was doing. He started singing "Some Broken Hearts Never Mend"—and her heart constricted. *My broken heart is healed—I'm together, whole. Yes, the memories are there. That's a good thing, to remind me why we can't go back, why I have to be tough, be my own person, follow my dreams.*

She closed her eyes and practiced relaxation breathing.

When Brooks stopped singing, he finished his glass of tea. "Austin, this is one of your Mommy's favorite songs. I used to love to hear her sing it." As he sang, "Daddy's Hands" she nearly fell off the swing. She held Austin's hand. *What is he doing?*

When the song ended, Austin said, "I don't have a daddy."

Brooks stared at her. She swallowed hard and said, "Yes, you do. You've just never met him—until now." The breeze stilled. Silence fell over all creation, not even a fly buzzed, everyone's nerves were hanging out their ears. She took Austin's face in her hands. "Austin, Brooks is your dad."

Chapter Nine

Austin stared at his mother. "I have a dad?" She nodded and squeezed his hand. He looked at Brooks. "You're my dad?"

"Yes," Brooks spoke barely above a whisper. He cleared his throat. "I didn't know until I saw you last week." His voice broke. "I'm happy to know you, Son."

"I'm glad you're my dad." Austin bolted from the porch swing and threw his arms around his father.

Brooks held him close, blinking back tears. "Austin, Austin," he said, "I love you, Son, my son." *Oh, God. I love my family. I love Katie, but this feeling, I can't describe it— my heart is about to pop.*

Austin pulled back and put his little hands on Brooks's cheeks. "Your eyes are the same color as mine."

Brooks laughed and tousled his hair. "Yes, and your eyelashes and your hair." He traced Austin's lips. "You have your mom's

52

beautiful, full lips." He held up Austin's hands. "Looks like you have Kane hands with those long, slender fingers."

Austin put his palm against his dad's. "You have big hands."

Brooks laughed again. "Yes, I have Travis hands."

Austin looked puzzled. "Travis?"

"Yes, Travis is my last name. I have big hands like my dad and Gramps."

"Kane is my last name. Like my Grandpa Richard."

The smile faded from Brooks's lips. "Yes, well, um, Kane is a good name."

Katie stood looking down at Brooks and their son. "I think we've had enough excitement for one day. Austin, it's time for your nap."

"Aw, Mom, do I have to?" He looked pleadingly at his grandpa and Brooks, but neither of them spoke. He put his little hands on Brooks's shoulder. "When can I go to your house and see your horses?"

"How about tomorrow?" He noticed Katie's scowl. "If that's okay with your mom."

"We'll see." She turned her son toward the front door and kissed the top of his head. "Go on in and I'll be there in a minute to read to you." After the door closed, she stepped off the porch and threw a sideways glance at Brooks. "I'll walk you to your pickup."

He followed her lead. She leaned on the driver's door, her back to her parents and hissed, "I said you could see him today. Don't try to push your luck."

He wanted to be sweet as honey, but he remembered his mother's advice about not being a doormat. He gritted his teeth to control the anger. "It has nothing to do with luck. He's my son."

"In a few weeks we're going back to Chicago. The more time he spends with you, the harder it will be for him."

He stepped closer and raised his hands toward her shoulders. The fiery darts she shot made him drop his hands and step back. "Did you hear what you just said?" He shook his head. "The harder it will be for him. Think about it, Katie." He ran his fingers through his thick wavy hair. "I know how much it hurts not to have a dad around, even though I knew I had a dad, and I had Gramps and Abuelo." He looked toward the porch and saw Richard Kane helping his wife inside. "You couldn't begin to understand how much that hurt, because you had both parents."

"My life wasn't perfect, and you know it." She kicked the dirt with the toe of her shoe.

"Katie, look at me." But she wouldn't. "Katie, I know you didn't always feel loved, but you were. Don't you want our son to *know* how much he's loved, by all the people who will love him if they have a chance?"

"I know how much it hurts to love and have that love jerked away from you." She swiped at the tears leaking through her eyes.

"Katie, I'm sorry. I never meant to hurt you. I didn't jerk my love away from you." He tried to touch her face, but she pulled back.

"No, you just walked away. And I do not want that to happen to Austin."

She turned toward the house, but he stepped in front of her. "I kind of see it the other way around, like you were the one who walked away." She tried to move around him, but he side-stepped. "I'll never walk away from Austin. Nothing, or nobody, can keep me from *my* son."

She brushed past him. He stood frozen, watching her retreat inside the house. He got in his pickup and headed home. Only ten miles separated Kane Lane from the T-C Quarter Horse Ranch, but he had to pull over. Overwhelmed with emotion, Brooks leaned his head on the steering wheel.

God, I can't imagine how you gave up your Son to die on a cross for sinners. I couldn't do it. I don't want to give up my son. I've lost out on six years of his life, I don't want to miss out on any more.

He took the red bandana handkerchief from his pocket and blew his nose.

I wasted six years of my life running after fame and fortune. God, I'm sorry I broke your heart. I promise you, I won't waste the rest of my life. The talent you gave me, I'm giving back to you. You got your Son back, to sit at your right hand for eternity. Will you please let me have my son, to be at my side? And Katie, Lord, I hurt her, too, and

I'm sorry. I'm one sorry devil. I can't undo what I did. We can't go back, and I wouldn't want to be a reckless teenager again. But God, if there's any chance for us in the future, please show me what to do. And please heal Katie's heart.

Chapter Ten

Katie found Austin lying in bed with his face in the pillow. "Hey, little man, what would you like me to read?" His only response was a shrug of the shoulders. "Okay, how about the illustrated *Black Beauty*?"

He rolled to his side. "Does my dad have lots of horses?"

"His family raises quarter horses. They train some as roping horses and some as cutting horses. Some are trained for all-around ranch work." She sat on the edge of the bed and brushed the hair off his forehead. "Your other grandfather, Dustin Travis, is a professional rodeo cowboy, team roping. Or at least he was." She lay down beside him and held his hand. "He's sick, like my mom. You have another grandmother, too. Her name is Carmela. She's one of the most beautiful women I've ever seen with eyes like yours. She's really nice. You'll like her, and she will love you. You also have two great-grandfathers, your dad's grandfathers, Gramps and Abuelo, which is Spanish for grandfather. You're part Spanish."

"I learned some Spanish in kindergarten. I can count and say my colors and the days of the week."

She smiled. "I know. I'm very proud of you. And now you know another Spanish word, abuelo, grandpa."

"Abuelo." He looked up at his mother. "Why don't you like my dad?"

She stared out the window. "I like him." Once upon a time she loved Brooks with all her heart. Before her heart was broken. She's not Humpty Dumpty, because her heart *was* put back together, but it's still fragile at the seams.

"Some of my friends' parents don't like each other, so they got a divorce. Is that what happened with you and my dad?"

She shook her head. "No, we never got married. I've told you that we were very young and we weren't ready for marriage."

"How come I never got to see him before?"

She pinched the bridge of her nose, trying to hold back the tears. She cleared her voice. "Your dad is a very good singer and guitar player. He went to Nashville to become a famous country music star. I went to Chicago to go to school with hopes of playing in the symphony."

"Is my dad famous?"

"He's been the back-up singer and guitar player for Canada

Jones, the Country Music Entertainer of the year last year. Some of their songs are famous, so I guess your dad is a little famous."

Austin sat up, his eyes sparkling. "Is he rich?"

She laughed. "I don't think he's rich, but he probably does have more money than we do, unless he's spent it all on the road."

"What road did he buy?"

She laughed again and ruffled his hair. "He didn't buy a road. I meant while he was traveling and singing."

"He sings good." He batted those long eyelashes. "I'd like to go to his ranch—tomorrow. I'd like to see my other grandparents— tomorrow. Please?"

"If you take a nap, I'll call your dad and see what we can work out." He closed his eyes and pretended to snore. Katie laughed and shook him lightly. "I mean a real nap. Let's read *Black Beauty* before you go to sleep."

***

Katie sat on the porch swing and waited for her dad to come in from feeding cattle. "Dad, could you take Austin to see Brooks and meet his other grandparents tomorrow?"

"I've got a lot to do tomorrow. Your mom has a doctor's appointment Tuesday, and then Wednesday I'll have to do double duty to catch up again."

"Austin has his heart set on going tomorrow, but he'll just have to understand that we don't always get what we want."

"No, we don't always get what we want, but it's nice to get some things we want sometimes." He sat in the rocker. "Brooks would probably be glad to come get him if you don't want to go."

"He can't go there by himself! He doesn't even know them." Katie stood and turned toward the door.

Her dad reached for her hand. "Sit with me for a while." He took his pocket knife and began whittling. "You know them, and you know Austin will be safe."

She shook her head. "I can't let him go alone."

"Then I guess Austin'll be sad. Brooks'll be mad." He stopped whittling and looked her in the eyes. "Or you can put on your big girl panties and take him over there yourself."

"Oooh! I hate that expression!" Duke laid his head on her lap. She patted him until Daisy came and nudged him aside. "Dad, you have no idea how uncomfortable it would be for me to see the Travis family after all this time."

"They may be upset because you kept Austin from them, but they'll be so happy to see him, they probably won't pay you much mind."

"Maybe you're right. Maybe I can just blend into the barn, hide out with the horses, or play cat and mouse while I watch my son."

"While you watch your son's happiness." He started whittling again. "They're good people. They'll love Austin as much as we do. He'll have a great time."

***

Katie took an apple out to Sissy and Peanut and called Brooks. "Austin would like to go to your ranch tomorrow, but Dad can't take him."

"I can come get him."

"I don't want him to be alone the first time he meets everybody, but I don't know if I'd be welcome."

"Katie," he paused, "my family's always loved you like their own."

She took a deep breath, trying to keep her voice steady. She didn't want him to hear her cry. "Yes," her voice broke, "but that was before…"

"Katie," he whispered her name, "It will be okay. I promise."

She wiped her eyes. *Come on, toughen up. Stop being a baby.*

"Katie?" He waited. "Are you okay?"

She nodded and then said, "Yeah. No. This is so hard."

"It doesn't have to be hard."

"I'll see you tomorrow between eight and nine." She hung up, threw her arms around Sissy's neck and cried six years' worth of pent up tears.

Chapter Eleven

Monday morning Katie got up before the rooster crowed. She took a shower, washed her hair, and applied her makeup with extra care. She put on a pair of white shorts and a red tank top. She took them off and put on glitzy jeans and a white shirt. She took them off and put on old, faded jeans and a blue tie-dyed t-shirt.

After breakfast, she told Austin, "Get your hat. We're going to the T-C Quarter Horse Ranch, your dad's ranch."

His smile spread across his face like the sunset on the west Texas plains. "Yippee!"

"Mom, if you need anything, anything at all, you call me and I'll come right home."

Donna took her daughter's hand. "I'll be fine, and so will you." She stood and kissed Katie's cheek. "I'll be praying for you."

As soon as Katie pulled into the driveway, the front door

opened and Mrs. Travis walked out, looking just as beautiful and vibrant as always. Wrapping her arms around Katie she said, "Welcome home. We've missed you."

Brooks sauntered up from the barn looking like a model for Stetson hats, George Strait shirts, Wrangler jeans, and Justin boots all rolled into one. He took her breath away.

"Thanks for coming, Katie." He removed Austin's hat and tousled his thick hair. "Gentlemen always remove their hats when addressing a lady. Austin, this is my mom, your Grandmother Carmela."

Carmela knelt down. "Austin, I'm so happy to meet you. You are a beautiful boy. Please call me Abuela."

"Mom, boys aren't beautiful, they're handsome."

"Oh, no. This one's beautiful, just like you."

As Brooks stood, the soft breeze blew his scent straight to Katie. She closed her eyes and breathed in that manly scent, a mixture of musky aftershave, hard-working sweat, and horses—so different from the overpriced aftershave, pretentious perspiration from an enclosed gym, and strong gourmet coffee of city men. Her stomach rolled, and she felt herself sway.

Brooks took hold of her arms. "Are you okay?"

She opened her eyes and looked into the deep pools of blue. "Umm, Dad's coffee was stronger than I'm used to. I guess it didn't sit well."

Brooks pondered her response. "You used to drink tea."

Gaining her composure, she stepped back and he dropped his hands. "Well, you know what they say—time changes everything."

He leaned close, too close, and whispered, "Not everything, Katie, not everything."

Dean Travis walked out of the barn. He put out his hand. "Austin, I'm your great-grandfather Travis. You can call me Gramps. That's what your Dad and his sisters call me."

Austin shook his hand. "Hello, Sir, I mean, Gramps."

Roberto Cordova knelt down and pulled Austin into a hug. Tears came to his eyes. "I'm your other great-grandfather. You may call me Abuelo," he said in his gentle voice.

Austin pulled free. "Okay, Abuelo. You have eyes like me and my dad and Abuela."

Abuelo laughed. "Yes, we have Cordova eyes."

Brooks tousled Austin's hair and gave him back his hat. "Hey, cowboy, you ready to work some horses?"

"Yes, sir!" Austin beamed.

As they walked toward the barn, Dustin Travis stood in the doorway. Katie felt his disapproving glare, and she lowered her eyes.

Carmela gently took her arm. "Let's go inside and I'll make you some tea. I have some of those peppermint tea bags you always liked."

After putting the kettle on, Carmela asked, "Would you like

anything to eat? Some toast or a homemade tortilla?"

"No, thank you. Tea will be fine."

"So, Katie, how do you like Chicago?"

"It's way different from west Texas." Carmela nodded, so Katie continued. "It's big and busy with lots to see and do—the symphony, of course, and theatre, and restaurants, and museums, and people from all walks of life, from all over the world."

"So, do you play in the symphony?"

"No. Well, not full-time. Sometimes I fill in or play for a special performance."

Carmela nodded again. "I always loved hearing you play. God gave you a great talent."

"Thank you. Do you play guitar much anymore?"

"Yes, more since Brooks is back home. Abuelo and I love to play and sing with him."

Katie smiled. "Austin is learning to play violin. He's doing well. With so much musical talent from both sides of the family, he can't help but be good."

"Neither of our girls inherited the musical talent."

"How are they doing?"

"Celina married a military man. They're in Germany. She teaches school, and they don't have any children, yet. Andrea is at Texas A & M studying to be a veterinarian. Austin is our only grandchild. We're so excited to get to meet him."

"I'm sorry you didn't get to know him before now." Katie took a deep breath. "At the time I thought I was doing the right thing."

Carmela handed Katie a cup of hot water and a peppermint tea bag. "The important thing is that we're together now."

"Mr. Travis didn't like me before. I bet he hates me now."

"It's not that he didn't like you. He was afraid Brooks would get married too young and give up his dream."

Katie drank her tea in silence.

Carmela took a large bowl out of the refrigerator and began rolling dough into balls and dipping them into cinnamon sugar. "I remember you liked my snickerdoodles, so I thought I'd make them to go with our red chili enchiladas and tortillas."

"Thanks. You've always been thoughtful and sweet."

"I love cooking, especially when someone acts like they enjoy eating what I fix."

"You're a great cook." Katie put her cup in the sink. "Chicago doesn't have enchiladas like yours."

"I saw on the news that they had a shooting in Chicago last night. Thirteen people were hurt, including a three-year-old child. They think it was gang related." Carmela looked at Katie. When she received no response, she asked, "Are you and Austin safe there?"

"We live in a safe neighborhood. Our apartment building has a security system, and we don't go out much at night. The school where I teach and Austin attends has an impressive, high-tech, state-of-the-art security program. We're probably as safe as we would be anywhere else."

Carmela nodded as she put the cookies in the oven. "I would miss the stars and night noises."

Katie laughed. "Believe me, you wouldn't miss the night noises in Chicago—the traffic and sirens—" She began making cookie balls. "I mean, you know, with that many people and that much traffic there are always sirens." Silence filled the space between them. The sounds of silence—nothing she experienced in Chicago.

***

As Katie poured iced tea in glasses, Carmela rang the bell on the back porch. "That should bring them in." She took the steaming pan of red chili enchiladas out of the oven and placed them on hot pads in the center of the table. "Put Austin's milk there, between you and Brooks. Abuelo and Gramps can sit on this side. Dustin and I sit at the ends." She put the tortillas on the table. Waving her hand, she said, "Go ahead, Katie, sit down."

Carmela motioned at one chair, but Katie knew that end of the table was where Mr. Travis sat. She moved to the other side of Austin's chair, the end closest to the kitchen where she knew Carmela would sit, so she could hop up and down serving her family.

Once everyone was seated, Brooks took Austin's hand, reached for his dad's hand and said, "Let's pray." The men seemed reluctant to hold hands, but they finally obliged. "Dear, Lord," Brooks began,

"Thank You for this food and for the hands that prepared it and the hands that provided it. Thank You for our family, especially for this wonderful addition, Austin. Amen"

"Austin, the enchiladas may be too hot for you, so I made you a cheese quesadilla."

He looked at his dad's plate piled high with the steaming enchiladas and said, "That's okay. They'll cool off."

Katie laughed. "Not that kind of hot. Chili hot."

"Here, Son. Try them with one of your grandmother's homemade tortillas." Brooks put a small amount of the enchiladas on a flour tortilla and rolled it up. "Since you've lived in Chicago, you've never had real Mexican food."

"I've had real Mexican food at Taco Bell."

Everyone laughed. "That's nothing like this. Take a little taste." Austin bit into his tortilla wrapped enchilada. His eyes watered and he took a quick gulp of milk.

"Don't worry. You won't hurt my feelings if they're too hot to eat. That's why I made the quesadilla."

"I like it." Austin said and took another sip of milk.

"What's your favorite food?" Carmela asked.

"Chocolate. I like chocolate candy, chocolate cake, double chocolate chip cookies, chocolate pie, chocolate pudding, chocolate milk, chocolate milkshakes, hot chocolate, chocolate pancakes, and chocolate gravy."

"Chocolate gravy?" Dustin screwed up his face.

"It's a recipe I found online. I make it once in a while for Saturday breakfast with biscuits."

"What other weird stuff do you feed the kid in Chicago—tofu, sushi, sprouts, snails?"

"Dad," Brooks didn't try to conceal his irritation.

"It's okay." Katie forced a smile. "I believe it's important to have a wide range of experiences so we won't be narrow-minded."

Dustin leered at her. "I bet you do."

Brooks faced his father. "That's enough."

Carmela stood. "Yes, it is. Today is a celebration for Austin. Who's ready for dessert?" She picked up Austin's plate. "I made snickerdoodles because your mom likes them. Next time I'll make chocolate chip for you."

Dustin stood. "If ya'll will excuse me, I'll step outside and have a smoke."

After the door closed, Austin whispered to his dad, "Should we tell Grandpa Dustin that smoking is bad for him?"

Brooks whispered back, "We've told him, but he doesn't listen."

Katie stood and started picking up plates. When she walked into the kitchen, Carmela said, "Don't pay any attention to Dustin. He's made many bad choices in his life. Now he's living with the consequences, and he's mad at the world."

69

"I'm sorry."

"I accept the choices I've made in life, and I live with them. Our marriage hasn't always been what I hoped it would be, but my family is more than I ever dreamed of. Austin makes it complete—almost." She hugged Katie. "Thank you for such a wonderful gift."

Chapter Twelve

For two weeks Austin spent alternating days between the Kane Cattle Ranch and the T-C Quarter Horse Ranch. He felt all grown up when his dad would drive up and honk the horn. He had grown to love all the men in his life: his dad, his Grandpa Kane, Gramps, Abuelo, and his Grandpa Dustin. Austin was the only person who could make Dustin Travis smile and laugh. Brooks said it was like his dad had a new lease on life just being around his grandson.

Katie's mother grew stronger each day. The doctor told them not to get their hopes up because cancer patients often experience a last hoorah rally before taking a turn for the worse. Donna said that Katie and Austin had healed her heart and God was healing her body. Katie enjoyed cooking for her family. She loved the peaceful quiet of the ranch, riding horses with Austin, playing violin with her father on the front porch. She tried not to enjoy Brooks, but seeing the tenderness and affection he showered on Austin warmed her heart. Austin's happiness was contagious, until she reminded him they would be going back to Chicago when school started. He said he wanted to stay in Texas and be a rancher. He could go to school with his friends from the Cowboy Church. But she couldn't stay. Part of her heart would always be in Texas with her past, but part of her heart was in Chicago with the promise of her future.

One Monday morning, Richard kissed Katie on the head. "I'm so glad you're home. That last round of chemo hit your mother hard, I wouldn't want to leave her alone. I've got so much to do after being gone yesterday. I couldn't get it all done without you and my little side-kick." He smiled at Austin.

"Well, we are here. I've made you a sandwich with the leftover chicken fried steak for your lunch, and I'll have a pot of chicken and dumplings waiting for you when you come in for supper."

"Sounds good. See you at suppertime."

***

Five O'clock came, but Dad and Austin didn't come in. Six O'clock came, and they still weren't back. At seven, Katie called Brooks and explained the situation. "I don't know where they were working today, and I wouldn't begin to know where to look. Dad doesn't have a cell phone, so we can't call."

"I'll be right there."

In a short time that seemed like forever, Brooks pulled into the driveway and Katie ran into his arms. He held her close and stroked her hair. "It'll be okay. We'll find them." He walked around studying the tire tracks. When Gramps drove up pulling a horse trailer, Brooks said. "It looks like they headed to the south pasture, but they could have turned off anywhere. I think if we split up, we'll have a better chance of finding them."

Abuelo and Dustin started unloading horses. Brooks opened the gate and headed south. The other three men rode their horses in different directions.

Carmela came to sit with Katie and her mother. Thirty minutes later, Brooks called. "Katie, I found them. Your dad fell in a gopher hole when he jumped off the pickup bed. Looks like his ankle is broken, and he's in a lot of pain. Call 911 so they can care-flight him to Lubbock."

"What about Austin?"

"He's a little shook up, but he's a brave little guy. He's been right here taking care of your dad."

When she got off the phone, her mother said. "Katie, I don't think I'm up to a trip to Lubbock today. Will you go with your dad?"

"I'll stay here with your mother and Austin." Carmela said. "I can be here as long as I need to. You go take care of your father."

The helicopter arrived about the same time Brooks drove in the driveway. He hugged Katie and said, "Go on with your dad. I'll be there as soon as I can."

Carmela put her arm around Austin. "Go on, Katie. We'll take care of everything here."

***

Brooks arrived at the hospital shortly after her dad entered surgery. "His ankle's shattered. The doctor said he thinks it will heal, but it will be a long recovery period." Katie's voice broke.

Brooks held her close as she sobbed into his chest, his strong, broad chest, with his stout heart beating out a message, "O-k, thump, thump, O-k, thump, thump."

She awoke with her head in his lap. *How did that happen?* The doctor stood before her. "Your father came through surgery well. He's in recovery. He should be in a full cast for six weeks. After that, he should be in a walking cast but shouldn't be on it any more than necessary."

"He's a rancher. It'll be tough to keep him down for even six weeks."

"If he wants to keep ranching, he'll follow my orders. I'll talk to him in the morning when I make my rounds."

When the doctor walked out of the waiting room, Katie said, "What a prima donna."

"I was thinking of another word, but I'm trying not to allow thoughts like that to walk through my mind," Brooks said.

"Independent rancher's insurance isn't that great. With all Mom's medical expenses, I don't know if they can afford to hire a full-time hand."

"Don't worry about that, Katie. I'll take care of everything until he's back on his feet."

He lifted her face and looked into her eyes. "I've decided to stay. I wandered far away from God and all that's important in life. I get more pleasure singing in the Cowboy Church than I ever did singing cheating songs about lost loves and broken dreams. I've found my way back where I belong."

She swiped her tears away. "Brooks, when school starts, I'm going back to Chicago." She took a deep breath. "With Austin."

He stood and walked to the window. The glare of city lights lit up the night sky, obscuring the stars. "We'll work out a visitation plan. I'll still be here to help your folks. They'll want to see Austin as much as possible, too." She could barely make out his soft voice until he turned to face her. "I've got some money put back. If you'd feel better coming with him, I could pay for your airfare, too."

"I don't have to go back for eight more weeks. We can talk about it later."

He nodded and walked to the counter. "Would you like a muffin and coffee, or would you like some real food? There's an all-night pancake house close by."

"I'm not really hungry."

"It'll be a while. We probably have time to go get something."

"You go ahead. I want to be here when my dad comes out of

recovery."

After he left, she walked to the window and stared out. The tears blurred the lights until it looked like someone had splattered white paint on a black satin backdrop. Like a piece of modern art—a piece of junk in one of those museums in Chicago, a depiction of disorder. *Nothing as beautiful as the night sky you've painted for us, God, everything in order, perfectly balanced, so unlike like my life. What am I going to do?*

Chapter Thirteen

Tuesday morning Richard Kane woke like a bull shut up in a chute. When the doctor told him he'd have to stay in the hospital at least two more days, he said, "You can just get a wheelchair and roll me right on out a here. I'm almost 50 years old, and I ain't never been in the hospital."

"You're lucky. We're administering antibiotics and morphine through the IV."

"Morphine? Well, you can take that out, or I'll jerk it out myself."

Katie held her father's hand. "Dad, please be calm. If it weren't the pain medication, you wouldn't feel well enough to throw such a fit."

He pointed at the doctor. "He ain't gonna make a drug addict out of me."

"Mr. Kane, please calm down. Your blood pressure was 160 over 98 when you came in last night, and the readings are still high. Do you take blood pressure medication?"

"No, I don't take nothing but an occasional aspirin."

"Pain can increase blood pressure. Your body suffered trauma and shock. What you need more than anything right now is rest."

"Don't tell me what I need."

The doctor walked to the door motioning for Katie to follow him. He closed the door behind her and asked, "Is he always this obstinate?"

"No, he's usually very calm, easy-going, and soft-spoken."

"He could be having an adverse reaction to the morphine. I'll order a sedative. Perhaps when he wakes up again, we'll see the man you just described."

Brooks walked up and heard the end of their conversation. When her father fell asleep, he asked, "Would you like me to take you somewhere, to get something to eat? I could get a hotel room so you could take a shower and get some rest." She raised her eyebrows and he raised his hands in surrender. "Just for you, if you want one. If you'd rather, I could drive you home so you could get some clothes or whatever you need until they're ready to release your dad."

"Thanks, but I don't want to leave him alone."

"Okay." He stood, his masculine presence filling the small space in the tiny room, and handed her a debit card. "Why don't you go get some breakfast? I'll stay here with him until you get back." She stared at the card, and he said, "I know you didn't have time to grab your purse."

"Could I borrow your cell phone so I can call my mom?"

"Anything for you, Katie."

She nodded her head and took his offerings. In the elevator she closed her eyes and prayed. *Anything for you, Katie. God I can't deal with that and my mom's illness and my dad's injury. Please heal my dad. Give him back his strength. And my mom, Lord, I don't want her to die. My dad would be lost without her. I can't leave him alone, but I can't stay here forever. I just can't.*

***

Katie felt much better after she'd eaten some fruit and yogurt and drank a tall Mocha Grande. She brought Brooks a breakfast burrito and a chocolate chip muffin.

"Thanks, Katie. Looks good. I can't wait to taste that chocolate gravy Austin was talking about." He stood, but she motioned him to stay seated.

"He's a chocoholic like you." She sat on the edge of the bed and held her father's hand. "Your parents are bringing my mom and Austin. I didn't think she should come, but Mom said she feels better today. They're bringing me some clothes and my purse." She lowered her eyes. "We'll be okay if you want to leave."

"No, I'll wait." She felt his scrutinizing gaze, but she didn't look at him. "This would be my day with Austin. I really miss the little guy when I don't get to see him."

"Maybe we should back off on you seeing him every other day—so it won't be so hard on him when we leave."

"I told you last night I would take care of things at the ranch until your dad is better. I promise I'll give you your space."

She nodded.

***

When Richard Kane awoke, Katie gave him a gentle pep talk. "Mom's on her way. I know you're not happy, but for her sake, try to be cheerful." She brushed the hair off his forehead. "It's just for a few days. Like you always told me, we can do anything for a little while."

"I can't be down for six weeks." He rubbed his face with his weathered, calloused hand.

"Austin and I came four weeks ago. Does that seem like so long?"

"No. In some ways it's like a dream, too good to be true. Other times it feels so natural, like you never left home."

She poured water in a mug and offered him a drink. "Dad, it's natural for kids to grow up and move away. That's life."

"Not always. Some of the Kanes moved away, but some stayed on the family ranch."

"I'm not one of them."

Austin burst through the door and flew into his mother's arms.

She hugged him tight. "Hey little man, I missed you."

"Grandpa Dustin and Abuela spent the night last night. We played dominoes with Grandma Donna. Have you ever played dominoes where you match the dots?"

Katie laughed. "I learned to play dominoes before I started school. Your dad was the domino king—nobody could beat him. He has an amazing, photographic memory."

Austin pulled back and stared into her eyes. "Do you like him now?"

"What?"

"Do you like my dad?"

She looked up to see all eyes on her—Dustin and Carmela, her mother and father, and Brooks. "Yes, I like your dad."

He threw his arms around her neck, nearly choking her. "Good! Cuz I love my dad!"

Katie stood and fluffed the pillows in the recliner beside the bed. "Here, Mom, sit down. Maybe we can get some more chairs."

Dustin waved his hands. "Don't bother. Riding in the car for two hours was enough sitting for me."

Katie took the overnight bag and a suit bag from Carmela. "Thanks, I'll just put these in Dad's closet. Fortunately I was able to buy a toothbrush and toothpaste, or I couldn't have survived."

After an hour, Richard said, "Donna, it's a long ride home. Why don't you go on now and get some rest. Katie, you go on home, too. I don't need a babysitter."

Katie put her hands on her hips. "No, I'm staying until they release you."

Donna shook her head. "Richard, she's as stubborn as you are, so no use arguing with her."

He opened his mouth in disbelief. "Me? I'm the stubborn one?"

Donna leaned over and kissed her husband. "Between you and me, she didn't have a chance to be anything else but stubborn."

Dustin waved his hands at Katie. "Why don't you walk your mom to the car? I'd like to talk with your dad." He looked at Brooks. "You go on, too. Women shouldn't be alone in that parking garage."

After they were gone, Dustin said, "What are we going to do about our kids?"

"Since they're not kids, I don't reckon there's anything we can do."

"I've made a lot of dumb, stupid mistakes in my life, but I'm trying to make amends." He shook his head. "Sometimes I wish my dad and Roberto would have tied me to a fence pole and beat some sense into my head."

"Nobody gains any sense that way." Richard reclined his bed and closed his eyes. "Some things have to come from the heart."

Dustin fidgeted with his hat. "I always loved Carmela and the kids, but I didn't do right by them."

"You're not the only man who's ever made mistakes. I should

82

have gone after Katie. I sure shouldn't have waited six years, but she's stubborn and has her mama's temper."

"Too bad about your ankle, but it gives us a little more time to give Mother Nature a nudge."

Richard raised his bed again. "If we start meddling in those kids' business, we're sure to make a mess of things."

"I'm not gonna' meddle. Brooks said he'd help take care of the ranch while you're down. Our generation doesn't like to accept help from anyone, but in this case, I'm asking you to stay down as long as you can and let Brooks help. Let's sit back and see what happens."

***

After their parents drove away with Austin, Katie turned to Brooks and said, "You don't need to stay, really. I'm a big girl, and I'll be okay by myself."

"I don't look forward to another night in that waiting room." He punched the button on the elevator. "I'll make you a deal. If you let me buy you dinner, I'll go home and I won't come back until you call me."

"That's not necessary. I have my purse now."

"We've both gotta eat. Then I'll go. Deal?"

She laughed. "Do have I have to cross my heart and hope to die if I tell a lie?"

He smiled, remembering their childhood promise. "No, I'll take your word for it."

While she showered in her dad's bathroom, Brooks closed his eyes and imagined what it would be like to be married to Katie, to have her and hold her until death do them part. *God, I still love Katie. I want to be with her and Austin, forever. I want to take care of them. She said today she likes me. That's a start—at least she didn't say she hates me. Six weeks, Lord, long enough for you to work a miracle.*

Chapter Fourteen

Brooks came the morning the doctor released Richard Kane from the hospital. Quilts and pillows filled the back seat of his pickup. "This may not be as comfortable as an ambulance, but it's not as expensive either."

The nurse and Brooks helped Richard prop his ankle up and fasten his seatbelt. "This'll be fine. I wouldn't want to ride in an ambulance."

"Austin wanted to come, but I told him his Grandpa Richard needed lots of room. Besides, he needed to stay there in case the women needed something. Of course my dad will probably be there." Brooks shook his head as he pulled onto the highway. "I'm beginning to wonder if we have a case of the body snatchers. I've never seen my dad act so nice and helpful. He dotes on Austin like he's some kind of super star."

"He is. Having a grandson is like discovering a buried treasure.

I know I've sure missed him the past few days. Being stuck in that hospital bed wouldn't have been so bad if he'd been there."

"Thanks a lot, Dad."

"No offense, Katie, but you suffocated me with your mothering. With Austin I *am* the *man*."

She turned in her seat and shook her finger at her father. "You need to be careful you don't spoil him."

Brooks said, "You've done a good job raising him Katie. Of course I always knew you'd be a good mother." She turned and stared out the side window, and he turned on the radio.

When Richard started snoring, Katie laughed. "I don't know how my mother gets any rest with that snoring."

"Has he always snored?" Brooks asked.

"I don't know. I've never heard it until I was in the hospital. My mother is too proper to mention anything that private."

"You snore a little, too."

She stared at him. "What? You've never heard me snore."

"Uh-huh. In the hospital waiting room. When you fell asleep on my lap."

She turned and stared out the window again. "I'm sorry."

He looked at her, but she wouldn't face him. "No need to be sorry. It didn't bother me one bit."

Did he have any idea how uncomfortable he made her? Snoring, or sleeping habits, was way too intimate a topic, and there was nothing intimate between them now, never would be again. Except that they had a son together. Even when she went home to Chicago, they would forever be connected with birthdays, holidays, vacations, visitation, graduation, and every other special occasion. *God it's going to be so complicated.* She reclined her seat and closed her eyes, pretending to be asleep, making sure she didn't snore. But then she did fall asleep.

The sun drifting through the window carried her mind back to a childhood memory, running barefoot through the field, playing hide and seek with Brooks and Andrea. Katie and Andrea, holding hands, ran to the tree and cried, "Safe!" Best friends forever. But in the dream, Katie turned and left her behind, just like she had in real life. Celina, who was only four years older, came to the field and sang, "Come home, come home. It's suppertime."

Katie kept walking, but the song played louder in her mind. She had given up everything to pursue her dream. But then so had Brooks. Well, at least he had kept in contact with his family. She opened her eyes and realized the song was playing on a CD. "Is that the Cowboy Church Band?"

He nodded and turned up the CD player. "We're singing that song Sunday. Sarah has a powerful voice, don't you think?"

"Yes, she does." She looked out the window again. "I've never heard Celina sing."

"What?"

"I've never heard Celina sing. I heard Andrea sing when we were kids, but I've never heard Celina."

He shook his head. "Where did that come from?"

She shrugged her shoulders. "I was just thinking about something your mother said the day I had dinner at your house."

He laughed. "Celina sings like my dad and Gramps. More like a cow bawling than singing."

She turned on him. "That's not a very nice thing to say."

"It's true and she knows it. She's a great cook, a great artist, and I'm sure she's a good teacher because she's always loved kids. Now that we have Austin, maybe Mom will quit bugging her about grandkids."

Katie watched the unchanging scenery, the view as flat as she felt. *They don't have Austin.*

"Do you need anything? I can stop at that truck stop up ahead."

"No, I'm fine."

"You snored again." He flashed her a sideways grin. "Not loud, kind of a cute little snore, like a puppy."

She turned on him. "Now you're calling me a dog?"

"No, I didn't mean it that way."

"Don't worry. I will make sure you *never* hear me snore again."

His face got tight. Glancing sideways, she could see the

muscles in his jaw. Good. Let him get mad. If he got mad enough, he would give up those silly ideas about them getting back together. Because they were silly ideas. Ridiculous. It would never happen.

Chapter Fifteen

When they arrived home, Dustin and Brooks helped Richard out of the pickup and wheeled him into the house. Carmela fixed glasses of fresh squeezed lemonade and the two families sat in the living room. Dustin and Richard talked about cattle and horses, the cost of electricity and gasoline.

Austin hugged Katie and his Grandpa Richard, but he was all over Brooks. He wanted to go outside and show off his roping skills. "Grandpa Dustin has been helping me. He says if I keep practicing, I can get a championship buckle like the one he's got."

"Mom, do you still have my old junior rodeo buckle in your trunk? I think it just might fit Austin." Using a thumb and forefinger, Brooks measured the small buckle on Austin's belt.

Austin's eyes lit up. "Did you win the buckle?"

"Yep, when I was about your age. You can wear it until you win your own at the county fair this fall."

Katie gave him a stern look. "The fair is in September. Austin will be in school then."

"He can fly home. The roping competition's always on Saturday."

She felt every muscle in her body tense. *Chicago is their home, not Texas.* "If you all will excuse me, I need to take a shower and change clothes."

"Mom, can you come out and watch me rope first?" Austin batted those long eyelashes. "Please?"

She forced a smile. "Okay."

"Grandpa Richard, if Grandpa Dustin pushes your wheelchair, can you come out, too?"

Dustin stood. "Richard, I can move the steer's head to the front yard, so you can watch from the porch."

"Fresh air is just what I need after being cooped up in that hospital."

Katie stood. "Brooks, will you help me refill the glasses?"

"Oh, I can do that so you can go on outside." Carmela picked up a glass.

Brooks took the glass out of her hand. "Thanks, Mom, but I think Katie wants me to help her."

In the kitchen Katie rattled the ice in the tray. Turning to Brooks she sneered, "Our home is Chicago. When he comes here, he'll just be visiting. And I don't appreciate you making plans without consulting me."

"Actually, he'll have two homes. That's the way it is when a child's parents don't live together." He began pouring lemonade. "I already told you I want to see him as much as possible. You saw how excited he is about roping and winning a buckle."

"He won't have a place to practice in Chicago. If he didn't do well, I'm afraid he'd be disappointed."

"He'd be disappointed, or you would be?"

She turned on him. "That is ridiculous!"

"Exactly." He picked up three glasses and allowed the door to slam behind him.

God, he makes me so mad I could scream. She splashed cold water on her face and followed him outside. Her mother and Carmela exchanged questioning glances as she walked past them. Her father's deep frown lines exposed his displeasure. Watching Austin's enthusiasm as he roped the steer head brought a genuine smile to her face. He had natural talent. Maybe he could win a buckle if he came back for the fair.

Gramps and Abuelo joined them for dinner. Dustin had smoked a brisket. Carmela made pepper poppers, fresh corn on the cob, coleslaw, barbeque beans, and her special chocolate fudge cake. After dinner Richard said, "I'm not up to playing, but a little after dinner music might help me relax. I haven't had a good night's sleep the whole time I was in the hospital with all those lights and beeping, buzzing noises. Every time I'd doze off, someone would come in and wake me up, poke on me, drain my blood, and then give me a sleeping pill so they could come back and do it all over again."

"I don't have my guitar," Brooks said.

"You can use mine. I've been playing for Donna in the evenings." Carmela went in the house to get her guitar.

"Katie, would you get your fiddle and play for me?" Richard groaned as he rolled his chair away from the table. She wondered if he did it for sympathy, but she agreed.

He asked them to sing "Donna" for his Donna. Brooks, Abuelo, and Carmela harmonized beautifully together. Richard then asked them to sing "Pretty Woman" for the three most beautiful girls in the world. After that Brooks suggested "The Most Beautiful Girl in the World," but Katie shook her head. "No, that's too sad."

"I used to sing that to you when you were a little girl, and you loved it," Richard said.

"Yes, but you changed the words so it wasn't sad, and you put my name in it."

He laughed. "Yes, the first time you heard the real words you got mad at me. You thought it was a song I wrote for you. Actually the words were for you."

"One of my favorites is 'I Can't Stop Loving You,'" Abuelo said.

Katie shook her head. "That's sad, too."

"Beautiful love songs are full of passion, the bittersweet emotions of joy and pain, like real love, like real life." Donna held her husband's hand and kissed his cheek.

Brooks played the chords and Abuelo sang in his deep, rich voice.

Katie closed her eyes and tried to concentrate on playing her violin, but she hit two sour notes. *Time has marched on. I'm in a different place. I'm not going to live in memories of the past. I don't love Brooks anymore.*

At the end of the song, Katie said, "It's been a long day. Dad needs to rest, and so does Austin."

"We're home now, if I need someone to tell me what to do, your mama can handle it."

Donna shook her finger in her husband's face. "Okay. It has been a long day, and I for one am ready for bed. Katie needs her rest so she can take care of us two invalids."

Brooks stood and stretched. "Mr. Kane, I'll be over in the morning to take care of the stock."

Austin leapt into his dad's arms. "Don't go yet."

Brooks hugged him tight. He tousled his hair and said, "You go on to bed and get a good night's sleep. I'm going to need your help tomorrow, Pardner."

After the Travis family left, Richard said, "I plan to sleep in my recliner. I can keep my ankle up, and I won't bother your mother."

Donna asked, "Don't I have anything to say about the matter?"

"Not this time." He struggled to get from the wheelchair to the recliner. When Katie tried to help him, he snapped, "I can do it."

After reading a bedtime story, Katie asked Austin, "Do I snore?"

"You mean those little noises you make when you're asleep? It sounds like the puppies at my dad's ranch."

She laughed. "Tell me about the puppies."

"They're black and white, and they have longer hair than Daisy and Duke cuz they're Australian shepherds instead of blue heelers. Dad says I can have one if we stay here."

"Austin, we're not staying here. When school starts, we're going back to Chicago."

"I like it better here than in Chicago."

"You can come for visits."

He rolled over and turned his back to her.

She kissed the top of his head. "Say your prayers."

He repeated, "Now I lay me down to sleep," ending with thanks and blessings for his dad and grandparents and the dogs and the horses. He didn't mention her. *God, he's only six. It's hard enough for him to understand without Brooks offering him a puppy.*

Chapter Sixteen

The next morning when Brooks knocked on the kitchen door, Richard said, "Come on in and join me for a cup of coffee."

"I've had more than enough coffee already. I just came to see if my little Pardner is ready." Like the perfect southern gentleman, he tipped his hat to Katie.

He looked so good in his worn blue jeans, the snug, blue cotton shirt unbuttoned too low for her comfort. She needed to set him straight. "Let's go out on the porch. I need to talk to you."

He stepped away from the door and motioned for her to go first. He raised his eyebrows at Richard, who frowned and shook his head.

When the door closed, Katie turned on him. "What part of 'we are going back to Chicago' do you not understand?"

He raised his hands. "What are you talking about?"

"Don't try to act innocent."

"What?"

"Last night Austin said you offered him a puppy if we stay here."

"I meant it. He loves those puppies, and every boy needs a dog."

"We are *not* staying here, and I don't appreciate you trying to turn my son against me by bribing him with a puppy." She pointed her finger in his face.

"That's crazy. I am not trying to turn him against you, and he's my son, too."

Austin came to the door. "I'm ready, Dad."

When Katie tried to hug him, he tensed and pulled away. "What would you like for lunch?" she asked.

"My dad smoked two briskets. Mom made sandwiches for us so you won't have to cook." Brooks put his arm around Austin's shoulder. "I'll have him home at supper time, but I won't be staying."

Katie watched them walk to the barn. When she went back into the house, her father motioned for her to sit down. "I heard every bit of that, and it wasn't pretty. You want to go back to Chicago, that's your business. This ranch is my business, and right now I can't take care of it. Brooks has offered to help out of the goodness of his heart."

"Out of the goodness of his heart?" Katie blew out a big puff of air. "He's just using this as an excuse to get to me and Austin."

"Now you listen to me, little lady." She stood but he caught her arm. "Sit down. This is long overdue." She complied and he continued. "I need help right now. Yes, I'm sure Brooks will do anything to be close to Austin, but if I was him, after the way you've treated him, I wouldn't want to be close to you. In fact, I'd run the opposite direction." He looked at her, his brown eyes reflecting disgust. "For my sake, for that little boy's sake, I'm asking you to be civil. If Austin can't have both parents together, at least he deserves to have two parents who treat each other with dignity and respect. How do you expect him to respect anybody if he doesn't see it between the two most important people in his life?"

"Dad, I don't want to encourage Brooks."

"I think you've done a pretty good job of *not* encouraging him." He took out his red bandana handkerchief, wiped his eyes, and blew his nose. "Your mother and I know you're going back to Chicago. We accept your choice. But in the meantime, can we try to get along and enjoy each other's company as much as possible? Can you call a truce with Brooks?"

"Okay, Dad. I'll mind my manners and be gracious, but that's it, nothing more."

"That's all I ask, nothing more."

As she washed dishes, hot tears dripped into the sudsy water. *God, I've held onto my anger for so long, I'm afraid I've become bitter. You promised that if we repent and confess our sins, you'll forgive us. I accept your forgiveness. I know I need to forgive Brooks, but it's hard. I loved him so much. It broke my heart when he chose country music over me.*

In her heart she felt God asking her how that was different than what she had done.

God, I told him I would give up my scholarship and come home if he would give up his dream.

Is that what you wanted?

Yes, no, I don't know, Lord. You said if we delight in You, You will give us the desires of our heart. We gave up on each other, but neither one of us fully achieved our dreams.

Delight in me and I will give you a new heart, a new spirit, and a new desire.

***

That night while Austin was taking his bath, Brooks called. "Katie, Andrea is coming in tomorrow for the Fourth of July celebration. She'd like to meet Austin, and I'd like to take him to the parade and rodeo. You could go with us, if you want."

"What did you tell Andrea?"

"Mostly I just answered her questions after my mom told her about Austin."

"I bet she hates me. We haven't talked for six years."

"I don't think Andrea hates anyone. It's not her nature." Silence hung in the air. "You were her best friend. It hurt her when you cut all ties."

She sighed. "Austin can go, but I better stay here in case my parents need anything."

"My parents would be glad to help out if you change your mind."

"Thanks, but I don't think so. Goodnight."

"Good night, Katie. Sweet dreams."

Yeah, like that will happen. She'd been dreaming of her childhood lately. Andrea had been her best friend, the sister she always wanted. She didn't have any real friends in Chicago. While attending the Conservatory, everyone she knew was either free and single or married. If they had a child, they also had a husband. The staff at school was cordial, but she wasn't close to anyone. The only person in Chicago she cared about was Aunt LeAnn. Chicago held her passion, the symphony. Her dream hadn't come true yet, but she was close. And one day she would find love with someone who shared her interests and goals.

***

After she read a story and Austin said his prayer, Katie told him he had two aunts. "Grandma Carmela showed me their pictures. One has dark blue eyes and black hair, like me. The other one has kind-a brown hair and light blue eyes like Grandpa Dustin."

She nodded. "Did your dad tell you that your Aunt Andrea is coming tomorrow and that you're going to go to the Fourth of July Rodeo?"

He sat up in bed. "Really, I can go to the rodeo? My friends were talking about it at church. I've never been to a rodeo."

She laughed. "It will be lots of fun."

"Will you come, too?"

"Not this time. I need to stay here with Grandma and Grandpa."

"Grandma Carmela showed me some pictures of my dad and his sisters when they were little. I saw pictures of you, too."

"Yes, we were very good friends growing up."

"Why did you stop being friends? Did you have a big fight?"

She shook her head. "No, Andrea and I never fought. We just went different ways."

"But you fight with my dad."

"I'm going to try to be nicer."

"Good, cuz I don't like it when you fight."

She hugged him tight and kissed the top of his head. "Close your eyes and go to sleep now."

She closed her eyes but couldn't sleep. Visions of Brooks waltzed through her mind. Waltzed. Oh, he was a good dancer. They used to sneak away to dances because her parents thought dancing was a big bad sin, right on up there with drinking, stealing, and killing. They believed it led to fornication and adultery. Maybe they were right.

She thought of Andrea, funny, outgoing Andrea, so different

from quiet, serious Celina. Brooks was the middle child in every way, except height. At six-four, he towered over his petite sisters. Andrea was a spit-fire. Kind and compassionate, she was a true blue friend until someone hurt her or someone she cared about. *The queen of grudges, she's probably spitting mad at me.*

She thought of Brooks, how good he looked today in his snug-fitting jeans and shirt. *God please forgive me, for my thoughts, for hurting my parents, for hurting Austin, for hurting Andrea and her family, including Brooks, especially Brooks. Please give me strength, wisdom, and a new heart.* "Create in me a clean heart, O God, and renew a right Spirit within me."

Chapter Seventeen

Sunday morning Brooks picked Austin up for church. Andrea sat in the pickup. Katie started to wave, but Andrea's eyes shot fiery daggers in her direction. "Mom, come say hi to Aunt Andrea."

"Not today, honey. Have fun at church and at the barbeque."

"Katie, our band is playing in town tonight. Would you like to come?" Brooks asked, hat in his hand.

"The church band is playing for the street dance?"

"No, a classic country band from Lubbock is the main attraction, but we'll be singing a few songs in the middle, you know, to get the message out about Jesus for people who wouldn't darken the doors of the church."

She raised her eyebrows. *My how things have changed, the church going out to the reach people instead of opening the doors for the right people.* Hugging Austin, she said, "Have fun, but don't talk to strangers."

"He'll be fine. My whole family will be there. They won't let him out of sight for a minute." He tipped his hat to her and walked away.

Austin ran ahead to the pickup. Andrea got out and twirled him in her arms before helping him into the back seat. When she turned back toward Katie, her glowing smile turned into a scowl.

Katie stood on the porch and watched them go. *Lord, if I could turn back time, I would do things so differently.* She sat on the porch swing and thought back to her teenage years. She loved to dance, even though her mother preached about the evils of dancing. Her dad never said anything. He sure has said a lot lately. Wonder what he thinks of dancing now? For three years running, she had been grounded for sneaking off and dancing at the Fourth of July Street Dance. Her parents never knew about the times she and Brooks danced in his barn. They didn't know that Celina taught her siblings and Katie to dance when they were in elementary school.

Now that she's an adult, she could dance if she wanted. But she didn't want to dance, not with anyone, especially not Brooks. She could be nice to pacify her dad, to make things easier on Austin, but no way would she get that close to Brooks. Never again.

She went inside to start the chicken and dumplings, her dad's request since he didn't get to eat them the day he broke his ankle. He sat at the kitchen table reading his Bible, with country gospel music playing in the background. "Is that the Cowboy Church Band?"

"Yep. They were good before, but since Brooks joined them, they're better than anything you can find on the radio." He sang along to "Wings of a Dove." He could play a mean guitar, but his singing, in his own words, "is fair to middling."

As she worked, Katie contemplated the words of "Thank You, Lord, for These Blessings on Me." *Yes, Lord, you have blessed me greatly. I've always had a place to live and food to eat. Money's not everything.*

Neither is the symphony.

***

Austin fell asleep in the pickup on the way home from the Fourth of July Celebration. When Katie opened the door, Brooks carried him inside. He followed her into her bedroom and laid Austin down, covering him with her lavender comforter.

She walked him to the front door. He took off his hat and said, "Thanks, for letting us have Austin today. He had a great time. My family had more fun watching him than anything else. You should have seen him dancing with Andrea."

She put her finger to her lips "Shhh, you know how my mom feels about dancing."

"In some instances, I'd have to agree with her. It depends on where you are, who you're with, what kind of dancing, and what else you're doing."

She opened the front door. "Good night, Brooks. I'll see you in the morning."

He stepped through the door. "Katie?"

She looked into those blue velvet eyes and immediately looked down.

"Katie, I don't want to step over the line, but don't you think Austin is old enough to sleep alone?"

"We only have a one bedroom apartment at home, but we have twin beds."

"If I pay child support, maybe you can get something bigger. Do you want to go to a lawyer and see what's a fair amount?"

"I don't think that's necessary." She looked into his eyes again. "We shouldn't fight anymore, for Austin's sake. He can come see you on holidays. I need to start coming to see my parents, too." He reached toward her, but she stepped back. "Good night." She closed the door and leaned against it. *Lord, why do I still get weak-kneed when I look into his eyes?*

***

Brooks was all smiles when he got in the pickup. "Katie agreed to let Austin come visit on holidays."

Andrea snorted. "So what? She doesn't have a choice, and she knows it. You could probably have him more than that to make up for the time she stole from you. Maybe you could even get joint custody, or full custody."

"What kind of monster do you think I am? I would never try to take him away from his mother."

"She's the monster—a cold-hearted, unfeeling, unconscionable witch."

Brooks pulled off the road and turned to face his sister. "It sounds to me like you're the cold-hearted one. You used to be her best friend."

"That's right," she sneered, "used to be her best friend until she went to Chicago and started hob-knobbing with high society symphony geeks. Then she dropped me like a hot potato, just like she dropped you, and hid Austin from us."

"I'm as much to blame as she is. She said she'd give up her scholarship if I'd come home and marry her."

"But she didn't tell you about Austin."

"No, but I wasn't ready to come home. It wouldn't have worked then. I'm older and things are different now."

"Is she still planning to go back to Chicago?"

"Not for six more weeks. A lot can change in six weeks."

"Yeah, if you believe that, you're setting yourself up for a heartbreak."

"Maybe not." He pulled back onto the road and started singing, "Heartbroke." When they arrived at the T-C Quarter Horse Ranch, he turned to his sister and sang, "Don't give up on believing in me."

"It's not *you* I stopped believing in." She slammed the door and left him sitting in his truck.

Lord, thank You for not giving up on me when I turned my back on You. I've never given up on Katie, and I don't want to give up on believing in her, believing in us, not now, not ever.

Chapter Eighteen

Monday morning, Brooks showed up bright and early, whistling a tune Katie didn't recognize. His tanned, clean-shaven face glowed with a light mist of perspiration. The blue plaid shirt highlighted his deep blue eyes. His snug-fitting jeans enhanced the muscles in his long legs.

Katie sent Austin to brush his teeth and asked Brooks to step out on the porch. He and Richard exchanged rueful glances. Katie closed the solid door as well as the screen. "Brooks, I'm going to try to get along with you. Austin can feel the tension, and it upsets him." He just stood there, so she continued. "It would help if you acknowledge that we live in Chicago. Let him know you love him and will see him as much as possible."

He stood twirling his hat in his hand. "Okay."

"Thank you." She exhaled a deep breath of air. "And one more thing."

"What?"

"Please don't dress this way."

He looked down at his clothes. "These are my work clothes."

"I know you're used to dressing for a crowd, trying to woo the women, but you're not on stage now, and I'd appreciate it if you didn't dress like this."

"Like what?"

"You know." He shook his head. "Yes, you do." He shrugged his shoulders. "Your tight clothes."

He gritted his teeth. "My clothes may be a little snug because I've gained some weight since I've been home eating my mom's cooking." The light dawned and he smiled. "Do my clothes bother you?"

She shook her finger in his face. "Not like that, Brooks Travis. I just think you need to set a better example for our son."

He couldn't repress the smile that spread across his face. "Okay, Katie Kane. Whatever you say."

Austin pushed through the door. He looked from his mom's red face to his dad's smiling one and grinned at Brooks. "I'm ready, Pardner."

Brooks put his arm around his son, and they walked toward the barn. He looked back to see Katie looking back at them. He tipped his hat at her and smiled. *That's the first time she's said "our son" instead of "my son." Thank You, God. I think we're making some progress.*

***

The next morning Brooks knocked on the screen door and walked into the kitchen. Richard Kane started laughing. "What are you doing wearing high waters?"

Brooks smiled. "I needed some different work clothes, so I borrowed some from Gramps. The pants may be a little short, but they're plenty loose enough don't you think?" He had rope tied to the belt loops like a pair of suspenders.

As he watched Katie, her face flushed.

Austin stood up and looked down at his jeans. "Your pants are even shorter than mine."

"Maybe we can quit work early enough today to go to town and buy us some new jeans. What do you say, Pardner?"

"Mom says I need to wear my old clothes to work in."

"I'm sure she wants you to wear clothes that fit well, isn't that right, Katie?"

She kissed Austin. "Have a good day." Over his head she mouthed, "Very funny."

Brooks laughed and nodded.

After they left, Richard asked, "What was that all about?"

She began running water in the sink. "I thought you could see and hear everything."

"Not everything, but I see more than you give me credit for."

She looked over her shoulder, and he grinned at her before

turning his wheelchair toward the living room.

***

Brooks called Katie at noon. "Austin and I are taking a lunch break. We'll be quitting early today to go to town and get some new jeans. We're going to go to Pat's for burgers, onion rings, fried okra, and shakes for dinner. You wanna come with us."

"No, I better stay here with Mom and Dad."

"We could bring them something to eat and you wouldn't have to cook."

"That's okay, I don't mind."

"Have you been to Pat's since you've been home? It's just as good as it used to be back in the day." She could hear the smile in his voice, teasing her, tempting her.

She closed her eyes to reach down deep for resolve. "Thanks, but I better not."

"Well, at least let me bring ya'll something. I could bring you a cherry shake."

It sounded good, too good to resist. "Okay. Bye."

"See ya, soon."

She hung up the phone and went to the porch swing. Closing her eyes she swayed back and forth, her mind moving to the past, back to Pat's, the only café around in those days. She could see the worn tile on the floor, the red vinyl booth seats, the chrome-plated tables and chairs. She could hear the classic country songs on the old juke box.

She could smell the tantalizing aroma of deep-fried comfort food. She could taste the thick, rich cherry shake giving her a brain freeze. She could sense Brooks sitting beside her, his muscular thigh touching hers, his arm around her. She could feel his soft breath as he leaned over and whispered in her ear, "I love you."

Her heart started pounding. Her head spun like she was on a rollercoaster instead of a porch swing. Her temperature skyrocketed. *God I can't go there. I can't go back.*

"Forgetting what is behind and straining toward what is ahead, I press on toward the goal to win the prize for which God has called me." *God, I can't forget the past, but I want to put it behind me. I want to move forward with my life, my goals.*

For which God has called me. *Yes, that's what I want. I truly do want what you have called me to do.*

Chapter Nineteen

Friday morning Brooks came into the kitchen. "My folks are planning a surprise birthday party for Andrea before she heads back to A&M. You're all invited, and they would love to have you come."

Richard nodded. "I need to get out of this house. I'm ready to go to church, and a birthday party sounds fun if Donna's feeling up to it."

"I love birthday parties!" Austin jumped up from the table. "Can we go, Mom?"

"Sure you can go, Andrea is your aunt."

His sweet smile slid off his face. "You'll come, too, won't you Mom? I saw pictures of you at her birthday parties when you were little."

She looked questioningly at Brooks. He nodded. "It'll be okay."

She tousled Austin's hair. "Go brush your teeth and we'll talk about it later."

When he was out of earshot, she said, "Andrea hasn't talked to me in almost six years."

"Well, then I guess it's about time." He turned his hat in his hands. "Austin wants you to come. I want you to come. My folks want you to come."

"But it's Andrea's day. What matters is what she wants."

"Really, it's okay." Austin came back and the two Pardners went out to work.

Richard asked his daughter to sit and have a cup of coffee with him. "So what happened the last time you and Andrea talked?"

"She asked me why I broke up with Brooks. I couldn't tell her the truth, so I told her the same lie I told you and mom, that I found someone in Chicago, someone in the symphony, someone sophisticated, refined and rich."

He frowned. "Are those things important to you—sophisticated, refined, and rich? Doesn't sound like anyone I know, or care to know."

"I thought that's what I wanted—to get away from the dust and dirt, to play the violin instead of the fiddle, to enjoy life instead of sweating from dawn to dusk."

With a pained expression he backed his wheelchair away from the table and said, "Dirty work, like I've done all my life?"

She reached for his hand. "Dad, six years ago I wanted

Brooks. I couldn't have him, so I dreamed up someone totally opposite from him, an image to fill my heart and mind, to push thoughts of him away."

"Did you find someone like that?"

"There are lots of men who are sophisticated, refined, maybe rich, but I haven't found anyone I want, not yet."

He nodded and rolled into the living room. She heard the cowboy church band playing on the CD player. She peeked through the door and saw him in his recliner, eyes closed.

No, I haven't found anyone yet because no one could ever compare with Brooks, in any way. No, he's not sophisticated or refined or rich. But, Lord, you know I loved him with all my heart. I thought I was over him, but seeing him again has brought back all the pain. And all the joy. And all the love. And all the passion. But my life is in Chicago, all my goals, all my ambition, all my dreams. Well, not all of them.

At noon her mother asked Katie to take her to town so she could get her hair fixed. "I'd like to go to church. I only went to that cowboy church one time and didn't like it much. Course you know me—I had my mind made up before I went. Your dad's happy, and he wasn't happy at First Church for a long time, too many preachers comin' and going, too much arguing over nonsense like the color of the carpet and who's going to be in charge of squeezing the money. Austin likes the cowboy church. I'd like us to go to church as a family while we can, before you go back to Chicago."

"Do you know they're having a surprise birthday party for Andrea Sunday?" Katie asked.

"Yes, Carmela called and invited me. I guess we need to get Andrea a gift of some kind. You have any ideas?"

"Nothing we can get here."

"I don't think I feel up to going to Lubbock, but you could take my car if you want to."

"I really don't have any ideas. Do you have anything in your craft closet you can give her?"

"You think she'd like an afghan?"

Katie laughed. "Maybe not. Let me clean up the dishes and we'll go to town and see what we can find."

***

At the beauty shop, they found a red and turquoise scarf with silver beads and a silver cross pendant. At the Western Market Place, they found a palomino Stars and Stripes Painted Pony figurine. "Austin will love giving her this. She'll love it because her favorite horse was a palomino, and red was her favorite color."

In the drug store they bought cards and paper. Katie found a card with a nostalgic picture of two little girls holding hands. On the inside it said, "You showed me what true friendship means." Later she would write a personal note apologizing for turning her back on the best friend she ever had, for lying to the person who held the other half of her friendship heart necklace, the person who had promised to be her maid of honor and her true sister forever.

On the drive home, Donna said, "I think we hit the jackpot today. See, you don't have to go to the big city to find something good. Sometimes treasures are right in your own backyard." She smiled, closed her eyes, and pretended to doze.

Katie shook her head. *Does she think she's being subtle?*

Chapter Twenty

Friday evening at the dinner table, Brooks told his family that the Kanes were coming for Sunday dinner. Andrea screwed up her face. "I wasn't going to leave until Monday morning, but I can leave early to avoid a confrontation."

"There's no need to have a confrontation. We've been like family all our lives, and we are Austin's family," Brooks said.

"I'll make arrangements to see Austin when you have him, but I don't want to see Katie again, ever."

She stood and Brooks reached for her hand. "Sit down and hear me out." She exhaled a stream of exasperation. "Please?" She plopped back in her chair. He took a deep breath and continued, "I love Katie. I've loved her since I was seven years old and she chunked rocks at those bullies to protect me. She looked at me with those hazel eyes, patted my face, and told me she would always be on my side."

"Another one of her lies."

119

"Andrea, the only lie she ever told, as far as I know, is when she said some guy in Chicago was the father of her baby."

"That's a pretty big lie. She cheated you, cheated our family and hers, and most of all cheated that little boy from the love we could give him."

Gramps said, "You two can argue if you want. We have to get back to work."

"No, this is a family matter we need to talk through. I'm asking all of you, for my sake and for Austin's sake, to forgive Katie, to treat her like nothing happened."

"But something did happen. Things will never be the same, and you're not using your head if you think they can be." The bitterness in Andrea's voice dampened the sunny morning like a dismal fog.

Tears pooled in Carmela's eyes, "Please don't shout."

Brooks rubbed his hands over his face. "You're right. I never was as smart as you, so I'm not using my head. I'm using my heart because I love her. I have always loved her. I will always love her. No matter what." He poured the last of the coffee in his cup. "Mom, would you please make another pot?" Looking at his grandfathers, he said, "You taught me to work hard, to go after what I wanted, to give my all and never quit, and that's what I'm trying to do."

He turned to his sister. "Katie didn't tell me she was pregnant, but she told me she wanted to get married, that she'd give up her scholarship and come home if I would. I wanted her to give up her dream, but I wasn't willing to give up mine. Yes, she lied, but if she had told the truth, I would have married her. One of us, or both of us, would have been miserable. It wouldn't have worked, and we would have ended up hurting each other and our little boy."

"She hurt you anyway, and I hate her for it."

"Andrea, you should not hate anyone." Carmela wiped tears from her eyes.

"Yes, she hurt me but not as much as she hurt herself. She took her mother's wrath, her father's rejection, and the shame of having a child alone, without a husband. She's sacrificed to follow her dream while being a good mother to Austin. She's still the same Katie, only older and wiser. And she still loves me. She may deny it, but I can *see* it. I can *feel* it. *I know* it."

"So you're willing to give up everything for her? Your dreams? Your pride?" Andrea shook her head.

"Pride comes before a fall. I chased my rainbow, and the pot of gold at the end was hollow."

"You've done good. You have a future in country music. Don't throw it away." His dad spoke for the first time.

"I've learned from you what *not* to do. You chased your dream at your family's expense."

"Brooks, do not disrespect your father." The coffee pot shook in Carmela's hand.

"I'm sorry, Mom, but it's the truth." Facing his father he said,

"Gramps and Abuelo were our father figures while you were following the rodeo, drinking, and chasing skirts. I would never want to treat Katie the way you've treated Mom."

"We all make mistakes, Son. Forgive your father." Abuelo's soft voice sprang from his tender heart.

"How can you say that after the way he treated your daughter?" Brooks did not speak softly.

"Because my daughter loves the man, and he loves her. Yes, he made mistakes. He rodeoed to make the money to give you all a better life, a life I could never give my family. This ranch is a legacy none of us would have without his sacrifices. It was hard on him to be on the road, away from his family, and he's paying the price." Abuelo sipped his coffee. "You must be willing to forgive if you want others to forgive you," pausing he added, "and Katie."

"Thanks, Abuelo." Andrea made a childish face at Brooks.

"You, too, Nieta. Bitterness will turn your beautiful face ugly."

Gramps stood and pushed in his chair. "I've had enough drama. I'm going to check the horses, and then I'm turning in." Abuelo followed him out.

"You're right, Son. I've been a failure as a husband and a father. The thrill of the ride—the cheering crowds, the buckles, the awards, the fame, the money—were addictive. Just like the booze and the women and the ranch. The more I had, the more I wanted, but it didn't satisfy." For the first time in his life, Brooks saw tears in his father's eyes. "Your mother has forgiven me, not because I deserve it but because she's a saint. I hope someday you kids can find it in your hearts to forgive me. And Andrea, try to forgive Katie, for the boy's sake and for your own." He blew his nose on his red bandana handkerchief. "Your mother never tried to stop me from following my dream. Sometimes I wish she had, but I would have resented her for it. Brooks, your life is your own. If you want to keep singing, shoot for the stars. If you want Katie more than the limelight, go after her. But if she wants the big city more than she wants you, then you gotta' let her go." He rinsed his cup and put it in the dishwasher. "Goodnight. I'm done with the day." He left the room.

"That family discussion didn't go as planned," Brooks said, rubbing his hand through his hair.

"I'm afraid nothing is going to go as you planned." Andrea began clearing dishes from the table.

His mother patted his shoulder. "Tonight is the storm. Tomorrow is a new day. Sunday we will go to church as a family. We will come home and have dinner as a family, one big happy family. The sun always shines brighter after the rain."

Behind her mother's back, Andrea rolled her eyes. She started washing dishes. Brooks took a dish towel and popped his sister on the behind. She splashed him with water. He laughed and said, "Some things never change," as he ducked out the door.

Chapter Twenty-one

Sunday morning Brooks felt as jittery as a bucking horse in the chute. He put on the patriotic red, white, and blue flag band shirt. All the songs they planned to sing carried a patriotic message, except one. Brooks wanted to sing "Amazing Grace (My Chains Are Gone)" and share his testimony. He dropped to his knees beside his bed. *Lord, fill my mouth with words that will honor you.*

He filled his mug with coffee and headed for the door.

His mother waved him back. "Where are you going? This is Andrea's birthday breakfast, her favorite, French toast with strawberries and whipped cream."

"I gotta go. We need to practice one more time before church."

"It's tradition to celebrate breakfast together on birthdays."

"Mom, it used to be our tradition. Dad usually wasn't here for our birthdays. Andrea and I have been gone most of the time the past six years, and Celina has been gone longer than that."

"That's why it's so important when we are together. Please, sit down and eat with your sister."

Andrea walked into the kitchen in her pajamas. "That's okay, Mom, let him go."

In three long strides, Brooks was at his sister's side. He tried to hug her, but she pushed him away. "Happy birthday, Andrea. I would love to enjoy your birthday breakfast, but I have to go so we can practice before church starts. I'll celebrate with you the rest of the day, and we can have breakfast together tomorrow."

Andrea rolled her eyes. "With Katie and Austin here, you won't even notice me."

"When did your eyes change from brown to green?"

She pushed his hand away. "I'm just stating the obvious. That doesn't mean I'm jealous."

"Good, because you have no reason to be jealous. You are my favorite little sister." He began singing, "Baby face, you've got the cutest little baby face."

"Mom and Abuelo used to sing that song to me because I was the baby of the family. It was a song of endearment. You and Celina sang it to tease me about being the favorite, the pet, and it wasn't nice."

"It is your song because you *do* have the cutest little baby face, and *no one* could ever take your place."

She waved him toward the door. "Go on. You probably need

125

all the practice you can get."

He put his hand over his heart and faked a wounded expression on his face.

Andrea laughed. "Just saying." Her expression once again became serious. "And don't worry. I'll be on my best behavior at my surprise birthday party."

Carmela gasped. "Surprise party? Oh, were you expecting a party?"

Andrea laughed. "Yes, Mom, we always have a *surprise* birthday party if we're home. You haven't been slaving in the kitchen the past two days for nothing. And the Kanes are coming." She kissed her mother's cheek.

"See you later, you party pooper." As he closed the door behind him, Brooks looked up toward heaven and said, "Lord, I hope this day is good."

***

Katie put on her glitzy jeans and belt. She tried on five different tops before she decided on a loose, white, open-embroidered sweater with fringe over a white, cotton shirt. She wore the pearl earrings and necklace Aunt LeAnn had given her when she graduated from college. She smiled as she pulled on her ropers. Her dad polished them to such a high gleam she could see her reflection. He had always kept her boots and shoes shiny. She didn't know the first thing about shoe polish until she moved to Chicago. Of course, she didn't know the first thing about a lot of things. But she had learned. Yes, she learned what was really important, and now she realized the most important things in life she learned before she ever started kindergarten. Things like love, loyalty, honesty, dependability, and hard work. All the qualities she wanted in herself and others, especially the man she chose to spend her life with, when the time came. Which wasn't now and wasn't Brooks.

Which quality didn't he possess? Dependability. He wasn't there when she needed him.

Did he know you needed him? Did he know you wanted him?

She looked at her reflection in the mirror. "He should have known I needed him. He should have known I loved him."

Austin walked into the bedroom. "Who are you talking to?"

Katie jumped and put her hand over her heart. "You startled me!" Austin backed up, and she knelt and wrapped her arms around him. "I didn't mean to scare you. I was just thinking and didn't realize I was talking out loud."

He threw his arms around her neck and squeezed. "It's okay. My friend Josh has an imaginary friend he talks to all the time."

Katie laughed. "I do not have an imaginary friend." She tousled his hair. "We better get you ready for church and Aunt Andrea's birthday party."

He jumped up and down. "I can't wait to give her the painted pony. And Abuela is making chocolate cake with chocolate icing and homemade chocolate ice cream. I've never had homemade ice cream, have I?"

She laughed. "No, and it's about time you do."

Later, when she brushed his hair, he asked, "Who do you love?"

She hugged him and sang, "I love you, a bushel and a peck, a bushel and a peck, and a hug around the neck."

He giggled. "I know you love me and Grandpa and Grandma and Aunt LeAnn, but when you were thinking out loud, you said 'He should have known I loved him.' Who?"

"Austin, sometimes you are too smart for your own good."

"Do you love my dad?"

She knelt and looked him in the eyes. "Once upon a time I loved your dad very much. But, unlike fairy tales, in real life people don't always live happily ever after."

"Why not?"

"Because." She sighed. *Lord help me out here.* "Sometimes people make mistakes. They hurt the people they love. What's done is done, and you can't go back."

"You could say you're sorry."

"I could say *I'm* sorry?" She felt the anger rising. "Sorry for what?"

"For hurting the people you love. For hurting my dad."

"Who told you I hurt your dad?"

128

He shook his head. "Nobody told me. But sometimes you're mean to him, even when he tries to be nice. You always told me to say sorry when I'm not nice."

Out of the mouths of babes. "You're right. I'm sorry. I will try to be nicer."

He threw his arms around her and said, "It will make my heart happy when you tell my dad you're sorry—just like it makes your heart happy when I do the right thing."

She hugged him. "You do make my heart happy."

***

After the band sang "Mine Eyes Have Seen the Glory," Brooks stepped forward, and said, "As He died to make men holy, let us live to make men free." He paused and surveyed the congregation. His eyes settled on Katie. "Many of you have known me my entire life. I accepted Christ as my personal Savior when I was thirteen years old, but I didn't live to make men free. How could I when I wasn't free myself?" He cleared his throat. "I was a slave to self: *my* desires, *my* dreams, *my* ambitions. God gave me talent, but I used it for my glory, not His. I woke up one day and realized there was no pot of gold at the end of the rainbow I was chasing. I had left everything and everyone that ever mattered to run after an empty pipe dream. The money, the bright lights, the fans, the fame, none of it satisfied. I came home, trying to find myself. I came here, to this church. I came back to God and His amazing grace. The Lord has promised good to me, but I was too blind to see what was truly good." He closed his eyes and sang, "Amazing Grace (My Chains Are Gone)". He opened his eyes and bored a hole in Katie's soul as he sang, His voice broke as he concluded. "Will be forever mine."

She closed her eyes, bowed her head, and prayed, *Lord, we are in church. He's supposed to be singing to you, not me.* At the intense clapping, she opened her eyes. The people were giving him a standing ovation.

Brooks wiped tears from his eyes. The band leader gave him a bear hug, and said, "Amen."

The band exited the stage, and the pastor walked to the lectern. He told his corny cowboy joke, prayed a dedication of the service to the Lord, and introduced the text for the message: John 15:13, "Greater love has no one than this, that he lay down his life for his friends."

Katie listened as the pastor talked about the sacrifices made by men and women to secure the freedom we have in America. He talked about sacrificial love of husbands and wives and parents. He talked about the great sacrifice God made, allowing His Son to die on a cruel cross to secure our salvation. And then he presented the plan of salvation.

Katie closed her eyes and prayed a silent heart-felt prayer, "Lord, thank You for Your great sacrifice for me, for Your amazing grace, mercy and love, for Your gift of salvation. Thank You for my parents. Even though we haven't always had the best relationship, I know they've always loved me. Thank you for the gift of Austin. Please help me be the best mother I can be so he will always know how much I love him. And please help me be nice to Brooks."

After church, Austin said, "Mom, can we ride with my dad?"

She hugged him, "You can, Austin. I think I should drive Grandma's car."

"I think you should ride with us." He raised his eyebrows and cocked his head toward his dad. "You know, what we talked about."

"I feel good today, Katie. I can drive," Donna took the keys out of her purse.

Austin took his dad's hand, and then he took his mom's. "Come on. Make me happy."

Katie couldn't help but laugh. How many times had she said those exact words when trying to teach Austin to do the right thing? "Is it okay with your dad?"

Brooks looked shocked. "Sure." He helped Richard into the car, put the wheelchair in the trunk, and turned to wave at his family. Katie looked back at her parents, her dad grinning from ear to ear, her mother smiling radiantly.

Austin sat between his parents. He waited until they were on the highway before he broke the silence. "Okay, Mom, do you have something to say?"

Oh, how our words come back to haunt us. She cleared her

throat. "Austin and I were talking this morning about how we should be nice, but sometimes we're not." She looked out the window. Austin squeezed her hand. She smiled at him and turned to Brooks. "I'm sorry I haven't been nice to you. I'm sorry I lied to you. I'm sorry about a lot of things, but not Austin. He is the greatest blessing of my life." She hugged her son as tears pooled in her eyes.

Brooks pulled off the highway, put on the emergency flashers, and put his arms around Austin and Katie.

"Group hug!" Austin exclaimed.

"Katie, I'm sorry, too." Brooks kissed the top of her hair. "I'm sorry I was too young and stupid to recognize the great treasure God had given me. I'm sorry I lacked patience and self-control. I'm sorry I wasn't there for you and Austin. But I promise you I'll never let you down, never, ever again."

Katie nodded, but drew away when she heard a pickup pull up behind them.

"My parents. They probably think we're having car trouble. Let me tell them we're ok and they can go on home."

He got out of the pickup and Austin said, "See, don't you feel better now?"

She laughed. "Do you remember everything I say?"

He giggled. "Only the good stuff."

Brooks got back into the pickup after his parents drove away. "Let's see, where were we?"

"We were and are on our way to Andrea's birthday party."

He looked longingly into her eyes, but she looked away. This is it for now. A giant step, teetering on the edge, on the edge of what?

"Let's go get cake!" Austin's face lit up like candles. Katie's heart was churning like the insides of an ice cream freezer, melting with each turn of the paddle.

Chapter Twenty-two

When they arrived at the T-C Quarter Horse Ranch, Austin bounced in the seat and giggled. "Open the door! I can't wait to give Aunt Andrea our present."

Katie fumbled with the door handle and moved out of his way. She felt like she just stepped off a boat, and the Texas sand turned to roiling waves beneath her feet. Brooks walked around the pickup and touched her hand. "It will be ok. Really."

She closed her eyes to fight back the tears. "Will you take me home if it's too uncomfortable, if I can't handle it?"

She turned and leaned into him, resting her head on his chest. He lifted his arm, touching her tentatively. Then he embraced her and stroked her hair.

She could feel the pounding of his heart. Gradually her heart beat in rhythm with his. She felt steady, secure, grounded. She wanted to stay in his arms until she felt his breath on her ear, and she began to

134

swoon. He pulled her closer and whispered, "Anything for you, Katie, anything."

She stepped back and said, "I just lost control. I didn't mean to . . ." She didn't trust herself to look into the deep blue sea of his eyes because then she would go under and never come up.

"It's ok. I promise everything is going to be ok."

She took several deep breaths. "Alright. I'm ready." As they walked toward the house, she peeked sideways. He was staring at her, probably wondering what just happened. *Lord, please help me through this.*

When she walked inside the living room, Austin rushed forward and threw his arms around her. He gave her the "secret" sign, and she bent down so he could whisper in her ear. "I saw you, and I'm happy."

She whispered in his ear, "Shhh, it's a secret."

He giggled. "I don't think so." He turned around and picked up the gift from the coffee table. "Here, Aunt Andrea. I can't wait for you to open this. You're gonna' like it. And I made the card."

She opened the card and read it aloud. "I love you, Aunt Andrea. I'm glad I get to be at your happy birthday party. Love, Austin"

She hugged him. "Oh, Austin, this is the best card ever."

"Open the present."

She opened it and said, "Ohh, pretty. I love Painted Ponies, and

I didn't have this one." She hugged him again. "Thank you. Every time I look at it, I will think of you."

"It's from me *and* my mom. Here's her card."

Andrea opened the card. She read the note inside and, without looking up, she muttered, "Thanks."

Austin took the package from his grandparents. "Here's another present."

She fingered the scarf and cross. "Thank you Mr. and Mrs. Kane. Red and turquoise are two of my favorite colors, and I've always preferred silver over gold."

"I'm glad you like it," Donna said. "Katie helped me pick it out."

"It's lovely." She still refused to look at Katie.

Looking around at his relatives, Austin asked, "Are there any other presents?"

The adults laughed. "Let's eat first and save the other gifts until later."

Austin took Andrea's hand and said, "I want to sit next to you."

"You've got it little buddy."

Brooks pulled out a chair for Katie. "You can sit here, lefty." He winked and sat at her right with Austin beside him and Andrea on his right. Her parents and his grandfathers sat across from them. She sat next to the end where Carmela sat, and his father sat at the far end of the table. Their parents and Austin carried the conversation.

136

Although the red and green enchiladas were delicious, Katie could hardly eat. Her stomach felt like she'd swallowed Mexican jumping beans. The chairs were close together, and several times Brooks's leg brushed hers. It could have been an accident, but it was no accident when his hand slid down her arm and took hold of her hand. It was no accident, either, that she didn't pull away because she drew strength and courage from his touch.

After the cake and ice cream, they moved back to the living room where Andrea opened her other gifts. Brooks gave her gift cards for iTunes and several different restaurants. "Thanks. This will help when I'm busy studying and don't have time to cook."

Abuelo gave her a hand tooled leather backpack with her name on it. "For my smart, beautiful neita."

She kissed him on the cheek. "Gracias, Abuelo. I love you."

Gramps gave her a new pair of red ropers. "Thanks, Gramps. I love you, too."

Her father gave her a card with two crisp new hundred dollar bills. "Thanks, Dad."

Her mother cleared her throat. Andrea refused to heed the cue. Carmela sighed and handed Andrea a square box wrapped in red and pink heart paper with red ribbon. Andrea opened the box to find a personalized scrapbook.

"I took a scrapbooking class at the community center, and I thought this would be a perfect birthday gift. One page for each year of your life."

Flipping through the pages, she wiped tears from her eyes. Hugging her mother, she said, "You're the best, and I love you."

"Pass it around so everyone can see it." Carmela stood. "Anyone want more coffee or tea?"

Sitting on the floor, Austin, Katie, and Brooks looked at the scrapbook together. "Look, Mom, that's you and Andrea holding hands." There were several pictures of Katie and Andrea, laughing, sharing life as best friends from first grade on. Until Katie got pregnant and broke all ties with Brooks. And the Travis family. And her own family.

"Thank you for a delicious dinner. I think I need to take Donna home so she can rest," Richard said moving his wheelchair forward.

"Thanks for including us in your family birthday celebration," Donna added.

Carmela waved her hand. "You are like family. No, you *are* family now with Austin."

Katie stood and took Austin's hand. "Tell everyone goodbye."

"Do we have to go now?" He looked pleadingly at his dad.

Katie remained firm. "It's been a busy day, you need a nap, and we need to help Grandpa Richard with his wheelchair."

"Aw, Mom, I'm getting too big for a nap."

Brooks stood and led Austin outside. "A gentleman never argues with a lady. I'll see you tomorrow, Pardner."

Dustin and Gramps helped Richard out the door and down the steps. Carmela and Abuelo helped Donna. Katie lingered behind the others. Facing Andrea, she said, "Thanks for letting me come today. I do wish you the best."

"Brooks thinks he still loves you." She shook her head. "Don't hurt him again."

"I don't want to."

Andrea gritted her teeth and glared. "Then don't!"

***

That night after tucking Austin in, Katie walked out and sat on the front porch. *What am I going to do?*

Her cell phone rang. "Katie, is it too late to talk?"

"No, I'm sitting on the porch swing looking at the stars."

"Can I come over?"

"No, Brooks, I don't think that would be a good idea."

She heard him sigh and hoped he couldn't hear her racing heart.

"I just wanted to thank you for coming today. It meant a lot to me and my family. It was awesome to see Austin so excited and happy. It was a great day."

"Brooks, I don't want to hurt you."

"I know . . . and I don't want to hurt you."

"Things could never be the same."

She heard a deep breath. "No, but they could be better, better than anything we ever dreamed of."

"I'm going back to Chicago when school starts."

"Okay. But always remember Somebody Somewhere in Texas Loves You . . . always and forever. Goodnight Katie Bug. Sleep tight and have sweet dreams."

The call ended, and her heart stopped. Tears blurred the stars. *Lord, why did he have to say that?*

Chapter Twenty-three

The next morning Katie called Brooks before the sun was up. "Hey, could you come a little early so we can talk?"

"I'll be right there."

A nervous giggle escaped without warning. "You can wait till it's light."

"I can come right now if you want."

"Ok. I want to talk to you before Austin gets up." Katie turned on the coffeemaker and waited on the porch swing for it to brew. When she walked back into the kitchen, she jumped and squealed when she bumped into her dad.

"Whoa, Katie, I didn't mean to scare you." He patted her arm. "I heard you get up. Are you alright?"

She heard a rooster crow and forced a laugh. "It's not often I'm up before the chickens." She took three mugs out of the cabinet, poured the coffee, and handed one to her dad. "Brooks is coming. I

141

wanted to talk to him in private."

He took a sip of the strong brew. "I won't listen in."

She added sugar and cream to her mug and leaned down to kiss her dad on the top of the head. "I'll be out on the porch if you need me."

"I'm good. I'll be right here if *you* need me."

She picked up the mugs. "I'm good."

"I know you are, Sunshine."

Brooks pulled into the drive just as Katie stepped out the door. Perfect timing. Golden pinks and purples painted the horizon, the promise of a sunny day. She stepped off the porch and walked toward the headlights. She handed him a mug of coffee. "Can we walk to the barn?"

He took a sip and followed her lead. She slid open the door and stepped inside. When she turned to face him, he bumped into her. He wrapped his arm around her before she could move away. His deep voice said, "The first time we kissed, really kissed, was in this barn. We came in from riding, I helped you down, you leaned against Sissy. I stepped forward and kissed you . . . like this."

She felt herself melting into him. Meteors lit up the darkness, just like the first real kiss. It felt so warm, so inviting. Somewhere she heard her inner voice telling her to stop, but the desire drowned out the words of logic. Finally he stopped and held her close, kissing her hair, and she could feel his hammering heartbeat against her face.

He kissed her ear and whispered in a husky voice, "I love you, Katie."

She pulled away and stepped back, turning away from him. She took several deep breaths, trying to gain control over her emotions. "This is exactly why I wanted to talk to you." She moved further away and stood in front of Sissy's stall. She reached up to pat the horse. "I promised Austin I would try to be nice and get along, but I can't have you telling me you love me."

He stepped up behind her, too close for comfort, so she side-stepped away from him. He put his hands on her shoulders and said, "Why not?"

She reached up and moved his hands. "You know why."

He put his hand on her arm and gently turned her to face him. "No, I don't know why. It's the truth. I have always loved you and always will."

Her voice broke, "Please don't. It just makes things more difficult."

"It doesn't have to be difficult, Katie. Can't you give us another chance? Please?"

"No. What once was never can be again."

"It could be even better. I want it to be. Austin wants it. And I think you do, too." He put his hand under her chin and tilted her face up so he could look into her eyes. "I think you still love me."

She closed her eyes and shook her head vigorously. "No. I still feel passion for you, but it's not the same as love. I'm wise enough now to know the difference." She walked to the door and turned. "Please don't say you love me, and please don't touch me again. I can't handle it."

***

He watched her silhouette, glowing in the dawn light like an ethereal being. His muscles quaked like a racehorse waiting to break through the starting gate. Thoughts swirled in his mind. *I can't deal with not saying it, not touching you, and I can't stop loving you.*

***

Her father sat at the kitchen table, the light illuminating his perplexed expression. She held up her palm. "Don't ask." She ran to the restroom and turned on the cold water in the shower. She wanted to wash away the scent, the taste, and the feel of Brooks. She wanted to wash away the passion in her heart.

Austin came into the kitchen just as Katie finished cooking breakfast. When he looked out the window and saw his dad's truck, he bolted for the door.

"Just a minute, young man, you need to eat before you go out."

"I'll be right back," he yelled over the slamming of the screen.

He found his father in the barn, hugged him around the legs, and said, "Come on in. Mom's got breakfast fixed. Bacon and eggs and biscuits."

Brooks bent down and hugged his son. "I probably shouldn't

come in this morning."

Austin stepped back and looked at his father. "Come on. Mom said she'd be nice."

Brooks laughed at the innocence of his son. "Okay. I am pretty hungry." *Let's see how nice you can be, Katie. I won't touch you. I won't say I love you. But I sure can be close, for our son.* He grinned as Austin took his hand and led him to the house. *The sacrifices parents make for their kids.*

As they walked into the kitchen, Austin pulled out a chair. "Sit here and you can be next to me and Mom."

Brooks ruffled his hair. "Thank you, Austin. Good morning, Mr. Kane. I think it's going to be a fine day."

Richard looked at Katie's back and said, "A hot one anyway."

Brooks laughed. "I do believe you're right."

She set the eggs and bacon on the table and sat down, staring at her plate.

Brooks flashed his best smile. "Thanks, Katie. It looks as good as it smells." *She may not look at me, but I sure can look at her, red face and all.*

"Dad, could you offer thanks?" she muttered without looking up.

Mr. Kane reached for Austin's hand, who reached for his dad's hand, who extended his hand toward Katie. "Mom, hold Dad's hand. We gotta all hold hands when we pray."

145

She scooted her hand forward and Brooks wrapped his around hers. *I wonder if this counts as touching. Not as much as I'd like to touch her, but it's a safe starting place.*

Richard prayed, "Lord thank you for this new day of life. Help us make the most of it. Thank you for my family. Please continue to heal Donna. Thank you for letting Katie and Austin be here. They sure have brought sunshine back into this old house." He took a deep breath. "Thank you for Brooks and his willingness to help me out. I don't know what we'd do without him right now." He sighed. "Please forgive us where we have failed you. Nourish our bodies with this food You have provided. Protect us and guide our thoughts, our hearts, our words, and our steps. Amen."

Austin and Brooks said "Amen" in unison. Katie pulled back her hand. He *accidentally* touched her fingers when she passed the biscuits and smiled. "Mighty fine, Katie, mighty fine." *Lord I do ask that you open her heart. Let her know I'm not just talking about the biscuits.*

Austin slathered butter on his biscuit and spread homemade peach jam on it. Taking a bite he said, "Mighty fine, Mom, mighty fine." The adults laughed.

Katie said, "Eat your eggs and bacon, Austin, before you get another biscuit."

Brooks piled bacon and eggs on his plate. "We have a lot of work to do today, Pardner, so we need plenty of protein."

"Protein?"

"Yes, sir. Eggs, bacon, and milk are full of protein. A working man's breakfast."

"Mom, can you pour Dad some milk so he can get full of protein?"

Brooks scooted his chair back. "Don't bother, Katie. I can get it."

She stood, almost tipping her chair. "No, no, don't get up. Do you want more coffee, too?"

"Naw, my temperature's high enough this morning without drinking more coffee." *She's blushing again. Good. She needs to know the effect she has on me.*

Her hand shook as she set the glass of milk on the table. Brooks took the glass to keep it from tipping, touching her hand in the process. She pulled away like she had been shocked by an electric fence. The coffee pot wobbled in her hand as she poured her father another cup of coffee.

She sat down and picked at her food. Austin said, "Eat your breakfast, Mom. You need some protein, too."

"I think I'll just eat a yogurt this morning. It's packed with protein, also." She stood and got a blueberry yogurt out of the refrigerator.

Austin curled his nose. "We used to eat fruit yogurt and granola for breakfast every day, except weekends. Then sometimes

Mom would cook pancakes, French toast, or biscuits with chocolate gravy. I like this working man's breakfast better."

"I don't know, Son. Biscuits with chocolate gravy sound pretty sweet to me. I can't wait to try them."

Richard looked from Brooks to Katie and back again. "Sounds sickening sweet to me."

Donna walked into the kitchen. "I don't know what sounds sickening, but this smells good enough to eat." As she sat down, Katie hopped up to get her a plate. "Katie Kane, why are you eating that processed stuff when you have all this good home-cooked food?"

"Mom, if I ate like this every day, I'd get so big I couldn't fit through the barn door."

"It wouldn't hurt you to get a little more meat on your bones," Donna said. "I'll be glad when I gain some weight back and don't look like one of those anorexic models you see in magazines."

"Katie looks fine like she is," Brooks said.

Austin said, "Mighty fine." Everybody laughed except Katie. She glared at Brooks. He smiled. *Yep, I've always loved that fire in your eyes. That and everything else about you.*

"I'm sorry, Katie. I didn't mean to hurt your feelings. You're still beautiful. I just like that country girl look with softer curves."

"You didn't hurt my feelings, Mom, but I'm not a country girl. Not anymore." She poured her mother a cup of tea. "If you'll excuse me, I need to go to the restroom."

"Thanks for the breakfast, Katie. It was mighty fine," Brooks said as she walked out.

"Mighty fine," Austin parroted. He looked around the table and laughed. Brooks hugged him, and they all joined in his laughter.

Chapter Twenty-four

As Brooks and Austin drove through the ranch, they came across a downed cow in distress. After examining her, Brooks said, "She's having trouble calving, having her baby. I'm going to have to pull it." Taking Austin by the shoulders he asked, "Do you know about babies, where they come from?"

The little boy nodded. "They grow in the mommy's tummy. Then the mommy goes to the hospital, and the baby is born. Are we gonna take this momma cow to the hospital?"

Brooks shook his head. "We don't have time because the baby is ready to come. She's going to bawl, a lot, and there will be blood. You might want to wait in the pickup."

"How old were you when you saw a calf be born?"

"I don't know about a calf, but growing up on a ranch I saw kittens and puppies and horses be born before I ever started school. It's different for you growing up in the city."

"I'm growing up on the ranch, now." He looked pleadingly at his dad. "Can I watch?"

"Yes, you are growing up." He hugged his son. "You can watch only if you keep your distance. Stand right here. Promise me you'll go to the truck if it bothers you or makes you sick. No shame in that."

Brooks got the palpation gloves and calving chains out of the truck. He put his arm inside the cow. "The calf is breech. I have to turn it."

"What's breech?"

"It's bottom first instead of head first." Brooks talked soothingly to the cow. The calf was already into the birth canal, too far out to manipulate. He clamped onto the hooves to try to prevent them from cutting the mother's insides. He planted his boots on the cow's rump and pulled. Finally it emerged, a wet, slimy, bloody mess. The momma hemorrhaged and heaved her last. Brooks cleaned the afterbirth off the calf, wrapped it in a blanket, and picked it up. "Austin, I need you to get in the truck. Do you think you can hold on to this baby until we find it another momma?"

His eyes got as wide as a deer in the headlights. "I, I think I can."

"Sure you can. Open the door and get in." He set the calf in the floorboard. "Wrap your arms around it like this and hold on." Brooks closed the door and drove toward the north pasture which held most of the cows and new calves.

"What about the daddy? Can he take care of the baby?"

"No, son, only mamma's have milk for the babies. That's the way nature is. The mammas take care of the babies."

"After Bambi's momma died, his daddy took care of him." Austin patted the calf's head.

"Yes, after he was big enough to eat real food, not just his mamma's milk." Brooks hit a rut in the turn row, and Austin bounced on his seat, losing his grip on the calf.

Austin wrapped his arms around the calf's neck again and said, "I'm not a baby any more. I eat real food."

"Yes, you are growing up."

"I want to stay here to live. You and Abuela, Grandpa Dustin, Grandma Donna and Grandpa Richard, Abuelo and Gramps could take care of me."

Lord, please give me the right words. "Austin, we all love you. Your mom has always taken care of you, and she needs you. If she goes back to Chicago, you will need to go with her. You can fly here every time you have a school break, including summers. If you have something special at school, or in sports, I can fly to see you. We will still spend lots of time together."

"You don't want to take care of me?" Tears formed in his eyes and his voice quivered.

Brooks stopped the truck and turned to his son. "I love you

more than anything in this world. I want to spend every minute I can with you, but I also love your mom. I hurt her before. I don't want to do anything to hurt her ever again. It would break her heart if you weren't with her. Think how alone and lonely she would be without you."

"I will be lonely without you."

Brooks hugged his son. "I will be lonely without you, too, but we can talk every day. Like I said, you can come here every break, and I'll come see you in between. I will love you always."

Austin sobbed. "I don't want to go. I like it better here than in Chicago."

Oh, God, my heart is breaking. "Austin, we have to be brave and strong. It will be hard on everyone when you leave, but it won't be forever. Please don't be sad, yet. Let's be happy and make the most of the time we have. And pray."

"Pray?"

"Tell God what's in your heart. Ask Him to help you be brave and strong. Thank Him for all the people who love you."

"I'm mad at my mom."

"Ask God to forgive you for being mad at your mom. We're supposed to honor and obey our parents. That's the fifth commandment, number five in God's very important list of rules." *And what about you? Are you honoring your father? Have you forgiven him?*

153

"I'll try not to be mad, but I'm still sad."

Brooks reached over and patted his son on the leg. "Don't be sad yet, Pardner. Let's be happy while we're together." The calf bawled. "Let's go take care of this baby."

When they came to a group of cows grazing in a nearby pasture, Brooks tried to introduce the calf to several cows, but none of them accepted him. He drove back to the house. "Looks like we'll have to bottle feed this little guy, so we might as well give him a name. What would you like to call him?"

"He's a boy?"

Brooks laughed. "Yes, he'll grow up to be a fine bull."

"How about Mighty Fine Bull?"

Brooks reached over and patted the calf on the head. "Mighty Fine Bull. I like that."

Brooks parked close to the barn. He took the calf from Austin and said, "Go in and tell your Grandpa we have a motherless calf. Ask him where his bottles and formula are."

Austin told his dad where to find the bottles and milk replacer. "Grandpa Richard said if he won't take the bottle to come and get him so he can do a track."

Brooks opened the cabinet, opened a new, sterile bottle and began mixing the formula. "A track?"

"Yea, a track tube down his throat."

"Let's hope he takes the bottle so we don't have to do a tube

154

down his tracheal."

Brooks cut an X in the top of the bottle, put some milk on his finger, and rubbed it inside the calf's mouth. He inserted the nipple, but the milk ran out. He put his finger inside the calf's mouth, wiggling it to stimulate the tongue, and the calf began swallowing. Brooks released a sigh of relief. "He's eating, Pardner, he's eating."

When the bottle was empty, Brooks put the calf in a stall with clean, fresh hay. "Let's go talk to your grandpa."

After explaining they would need to feed the calf one quart of milk substitute three times a day for a few months, Mr. Kane said, "Austin, if you can feed him and take care of him, you can have him. He'll be your bull, the start of your own herd."

"I can do that! My own calf! Yippee!"

"Right now go in the bathroom and get those dirty clothes off so you can take a shower. I'm sure your dad needs to go home and clean up, also." Katie turned him toward the bathroom and gently swatted his behind. Once he was in the bathroom, she turned to Brooks and said, "First you promise him a puppy, and you," shaking her head at her father she gritted her teeth, "you promise him a bull and a herd of cattle." She exhaled a puff of exasperated steam. "Stop conspiring against me."

Watching her storm down the hall, Richard said, "If she were a fire-breathing dragon, we'd both be burned to a crisp."

Brooks shook his head. "Are you sure she's not, because I feel like I've been charbroiled."

"She is a spit-fire, just like her mama. It keeps life lively." Mr. Kane started laughing. "Don't worry, Son, she'll cool down."

"I hope so." Brooks looked down at his clothes. "I'll go drag that cow to the bone pile before I go home and clean up."

"No need to come back after that. It's already been a long day." Mr. Kane winked. "I'll tell Katie to help Austin feed the calf this evening."

Brooks wrinkled his brow. "Are you sure she'll do it."

"Over the years she bottle fed lots of calves. Regardless of how tough she acts, she has a tender heart. Feeding a baby might be what she needs to get back in touch with who she really is."

Chapter Twenty-five

As Austin dressed, he told his mother all about the calf being born, the mama dying, trying to find another cow to nurse it, and bottle feeding. "I named him Mighty Fine Bull. And he's mine, all mine."

"Austin, bulls aren't like puppies. They will bond with whoever feeds them, but once they're weaned and introduced back into the herd, their natural instincts take over. Bulls are not pets. They grow to be big and strong and can be dangerous."

"How long will I need to feed him?

"He will need a bottle for 60-90 days." She cleaned out the tub. "Grandpa's ankle will be well in a few weeks. He can take over the feeding when we go back to Chicago."

Austin's mouth puckered into a pout. "I like it here. I like living in Texas, on a ranch, with animals. I don't want to go back to Chicago. Can't we stay here?"

"We live in Chicago. That's where I work, where you go to

school."

"I could live here, go to school here, and go to the cowboy church. And you could come visit me."

His words pierced her heart. "You've had an exciting day. Why don't you lie down while I cook dinner?"

"Do I have to?"

"I think that would be good. Rest now so you can feed your calf later this evening."

***

Her father came into the kitchen as she made salad to go along with the chicken crescents. Richard raised his eyebrows. "The way you're whacking that knife around, I'm glad I'm not a carrot."

She waved the knife in the air. "I hope you and Brooks are happy. Between the horses, the dogs, the puppy, and the bull, he doesn't want to go back to Chicago. He said he could stay here and I could come visit him."

Richard sipped his sweet tea and waited for Katie to resume her chopping. "Maybe it's not just the animals. Maybe he likes the love and attention he gets from family."

She dumped the carrots into the salad bowl and attacked the cucumber. "We are a family. Austin and me. Everyone else is extended family. Extra family. Not essential."

Richard took another sip of his tea. "I always thought, as your father, I was an essential part of your life."

She dumped the cucumber in the bowl and sliced the onion. Wiping tears from her eyes she said, "Yes, but when I was growing up, you were always there, not some afterthought."

He took another sip of tea. "If you put a piece of saltine cracker in your mouth, that onion won't make your eyes water."

She wiped her eyes on her sleeve. Waving the knife in the air, she said, "You think this is from the onion. My heart is breaking here. I don't want to lose my son."

"Your heart is not the only one that's breaking." He set his glass on the table and turned his wheelchair toward the door. "Sounds like a no-win situation."

"It could be a win-win situation if you all would help me instead of working against me. It is normal for adults to move away from their family, and it is natural for a child to be with his mother. He can come here to visit, like normal kids visit their grandparents, occasionally." She stared at her father's retreating back, the only response the buzzing of the wheelchair motor.

***

At dinner, Austin bubbled with excitement as he told his grandparents about his day. "I named *my* bull Mighty Fine Bull."

"I think that's a mighty fine name," Richard told his grandson.

"Oh, my, when your mama was a little girl, she loved animals. She raised a bull one year for 4-H. Won the blue ribbon at the county fair, but she didn't want to sell him. We kept him, and he turned out to be the orneriest bull I ever saw. He wasn't satisfied with our cows. He broke through fences and went visiting the neighbors' cows." Donna shook her head and clucked her tongue. "When he killed the neighbor's bull, we had to sell him."

Austin's blue eyes got stormy. His grandpa said, "You don't need to be afraid of Mighty Fine. While he's on the bottle, he'll be just a big old lovable baby. Most bulls are manageable. Your mama's bull, Old Senator, was just plain evil, like most politicians."

"What's a politician?"

Richard looked his grandson square in the eye. "A politician is someone who says one thing to get elected and then does just the opposite after they're in office."

Katie shook her head when her father started to elaborate. "Politicians are public servants, like councilmen, mayors, senators, and the President. Eat your dinner so we can feed Mighty Fine before bedtime."

***

Katie mixed up the milk and handed Austin the bottle. "You ready to feed Mighty Fine?"

"Yes, ma'am."

Katie opened the stall, rubbed the calf on the head, straddling his back while holding his head. "Squirt some milk on your fingers and rub it on his lips so he'll know what you have."

Austin followed instructions and then held the bottle while the calf ate.

"Pet him and rub on him so he can get your scent, learn who you are."

"How old were you were when you raised your bull?"

Katie cocked her head and counted on her fingers. "Let's see, I guess I was 13. Before that I raised rabbits and goats. Senator was the only bull I raised. He was hard to handle by the time he was old enough to show." She led Austin out of the stall and closed the gate. "I raised rabbits one more year. After that, I concentrated on my music so I could get a scholarship and play in the symphony. That's all I dreamed about."

"Did you dream the same dream every night?"

"No, it was more like a daytime dream, a goal. It's all I thought about, all I wanted. So I worked really hard, put all my effort into becoming the best violinist I could be." *It wasn't all I wanted or thought about. Every night I fell asleep dreaming of Brooks, even after I moved to Chicago.*

"Your dream came true because sometimes you play in the symphony."

She nodded yes, while her heart cried no. She showed Austin how to wash the bottle and nipple. "Let's go in and get you ready for bed."

After he said his prayers, Katie said, "Sleep tight and have sweet dreams."

"You know what my daytime dream is?"

She had a good idea but didn't really want to hear it. "What is your daytime dream?"

"I dream of a big house with a big porch all the way around, with rocking chairs and swings, and a barn and puppies, with horses in one pasture and cows in another pasture."

She nodded. "Do you live in the big house?"

"Yes. With you." She kissed him on the top of the head. He took a deep breath and continued. "And with my dad, and a brother, and a sister. And all the grandparents come to our house and play and sing on the porch. And we eat chocolate cake and homemade ice cream."

It was a pleasant image even though it would never happen. "Maybe all the grandparents can come over one night this week, and we can sit on the porch and play and sing. How would you like that?"

"That would make my heart happy." He threw his arms around her neck and hugged her. "And don't forget the chocolate cake and ice cream."

Chapter Twenty-six

The next morning, Katie woke Austin up before dawn. "Hey, little man. Mighty Fine is waiting on his breakfast." They could hear the calf bawling before they opened the barn door.

"Sounds like he's really hungry," Austin said rushing to the stall.

"You go ahead and love on him, while I fix the bottle." Katie heard the pickup pull into the driveway. *Lord, give me strength.*

Brooks strolled into the barn with his long, smooth stride. He looked like a young Tom Selleck: his wet, black hair curling on his forehead, his violet eyes gleaming like a moonlit night, his smile shining as bright as the West Texas sun. Katie's breath caught in her throat, and she gasped.

"I'm sorry, Katie. I didn't mean to startle you." His smile faded.

She felt herself flush. If only he knew how much he disturbed her. She cleared her throat. "It's okay. I wasn't expecting you so early."

"I brought a halter for Mighty Fine. I thought it would be easier to feed him." He put the halter on the calf. "Do you want to help Austin feed him, or do you want me to do it?"

"Now that you're here, you can do it." She handed him the warm bottle, hoping he couldn't feel the heat radiating from deep inside her. "I'll go on in and cook breakfast."

She looked at her reflection in the mirror as she washed her hands. *Why is it men, at least Brooks, can look so good naturally while women have to spend hours on their hair, their makeup, their clothes, and their hands?* She applied some makeup and adjusted her ponytail. She added lip gloss, because her lips were dry. *Yeah, that's the reason.*

***

While they washed the bottle, Austin told his dad about his daytime dream. "Better not tell your mom about that dream just yet."

"I already did, last night."

Brooks raised his eyebrows. "What did she say?"

"She said maybe all the grandparents and you can come over one night and we can sing and play on the porch and eat chocolate cake and homemade ice cream."

"What?" Brooks dried his hands and stooped to eye level with his son. "She said that after you told her your daytime dream?"

"That's what she said."

"And you told her the part about the brother and sister?"

"Yep, sure did."

Two more kids. That's better than my dream. Brooks stood and ruffled his son's hair. "Let's go on in and eat breakfast before we muck the stalls and get all smelly."

When they entered the kitchen, Brooks said, "Austin, you go on and wash your face and hands, brush your teeth and hair before breakfast." He sat down at the table.

Katie dropped the spatula.

"Am I making you nervous?" he asked in his slow, deep, drawl.

She spun around and glared at him. "Stop staring at me."

He smiled. "Your back is turned. You can't see me."

"I can feel you."

He laughed. "You can feel my eyes watching you?"

She picked up the spatula, turned on the water, and began washing it. "I could always feel you watching me."

"Yes, but you used to like it." She could hear the smile in his voice.

"Used to is correct." She continued to rub the spatula.

"I think that's probably clean." He stood and took a step toward her.

She turned waving the spatula in the air. "You can go on back to the barn, and I'll call you when breakfast is ready."

165

Austin returned to the kitchen. Looking from one parent to the other he said, "We're waiting to muck the barn because we didn't want to get dirty and stinky before breakfast."

Richard rolled his wheelchair into the kitchen. "Katie, could you please pour me a cup of coffee? I'd like to sit on the porch and enjoy the sunrise."

"I think I'll join you," Brooks said.

Katie handed her father a cup of coffee. Turning her back to him, she asked Brooks, "Would you like one, too?"

"Thank you, Katie, that would be right nice."

She handed him a cup, avoiding his eyes. "Austin, would you like to go out on the porch with the men? You may have a glass of milk or orange juice."

He batted his long lashes and smiled. "Can I have some coffee?"

Brooks laughed. "Not until you're old enough to shave, young man."

Austin rubbed his chin. "When do you think I'll be old enough?"

Brooks smiled and ruffled his hair. "Not for a few years. Maybe when you're fifteen or sixteen."

Katie shook her head and rolled her eyes. "Would you like some chocolate syrup in your milk?"

"Yeah!" Brooks looked at his son with raised eyebrows, so

Austin corrected himself. "Yes, ma'am."

***

When the men came in for breakfast, Austin organized the seating arrangement so that Brooks and Katie had to hold hands during the prayer. He caressed her hand with his thumb. When she tried to pull away, he held tight and didn't let go until after Richard said amen.

"Dad, last night Mom said all the grandparents could come over to play and sing on the porch, and we could eat chocolate cake and ice cream."

"Austin, please don't talk with food in your mouth," Katie admonished him.

Richard made a show of swallowing. "I think that sounds like a fine idea. When do you want to do it?"

"Do what?" Donna asked as she entered the kitchen.

Katie got up to pour her mother a cup of tea. "Austin would like his family, all of his family, to come over and sing and play on the porch."

"Don't forget the chocolate cake and ice cream," Austin added.

Donna clapped her hands together. "Oh, I think that's a lovely idea! Can we do it tomorrow? I have my last chemo treatment on Thursday, and I won't feel worth anything for a few days afterwards."

"I'll call Carmela and invite them," Katie said forcing a smile. *Oh Lord, why did I open my big mouth?*

"Abuelo was talking about butchering a goat. We could have

barbequed cabrito," Brooks offered.

"Barbequed goat? You eat goat? You . . . kill them?" Austin asked.

"Yes, Austin. It's not much different than eating beef, which comes from cows. When Abuelo smokes cabrito, it's delicious," Katie explained.

"We're ranchers. We eat meat. When your mom buys meat at the grocery store or at a restaurant, someone raised the cow or the pig or the chicken for food. Someone killed it, and someone cooks it. That's how we live," Richard said, giving Katie one of those 'see what you've done to the kid' looks.

"I would love some of Abuelo's cabrito. It's been so long." Katie closed her eyes, remembering her last barbeque at the T-C Quarter Horse Ranch before going to college. Sitting around the open fire, laughing, singing, Brooks with his arm around her, kissing her, whispering in her ear, leading her away, where it happened—the night they conceived Austin. She trembled, her eyes popped open. She felt the heat coursing through her body, up her neck, flooding her face.

She looked at Brooks, whose blue eyes could see right through her. *He knows what I was thinking. He remembers, too.* She scooted her chair back, and staggered to her feet.

Donna's pale face became ashen. "Katie, are you alright."

"I . . . I need to go to the restroom." She rushed down the hall, closed the door, and slid to the floor. Head in her hands she prayed,

Lord, please help me. I can't think about what happened, especially not with Brooks in the same room. I've asked you to forgive me for my sin. I don't want to make the same mistake, but I'm weak. I can't stay here. I have to get away, away from Books.

She stayed in the restroom long enough for everyone to finish eating. When she returned to the kitchen, she found her mother washing dishes. "Here, Mom, let me do those."

"I'm almost done." Donna rinsed the last pan and placed it in the dish drainer. "Please have a cup of tea with me."

Sitting at the table, her mother said, "Brooks called his mother right after breakfast. Abuelo will bring the cabrito, Carmela said she'll make the chocolate cake and ice cream. I can make baked beans and potato salad. What else would you like to have?"

"I don't know." Katie shrugged. "A tossed salad, fresh green beans with new potatoes, maybe your cornbread salad. I don't know how to make that. I could make peach cobbler for dad since he's not crazy about chocolate."

Her mother reached across the table and patted her hand. "Are you ok?"

She shrugged again.

"You looked ill when you left the table."

"I'm not sick. It's just hard, the memories, the regrets." She took her cup to the dishwasher and dabbed her eyes with a paper towel.

169

"Could you pour me another cup of tea?" When Katie complied, her mother said, "Please sit down so we can talk."

Katie fidgeted with the paper towel in her hand. "I have to go back to Chicago before school starts."

Donna sipped her tea. "If that's what will make you truly happy, then that's what you should do."

"Austin is happy here. He wants to stay here . . . without me." She crumpled and uncrumpled the paper towel.

"I'm sure he doesn't want to stay without you." Donna sipped her tea. "He's a child. This is a new experience, a whole new world for him."

Katie sighed. "I thought Chicago was a whole new world, *the* world, exciting, liberating. I thought the symphony would carry me away from the wind and dirt, the cattle and hard work. Everyone here, my music teachers in Lubbock, bragged about my natural talent. I thought it would be so easy, but it wasn't."

"You also had a child, which made the goal more difficult to achieve."

"He's the only reason I stuck it out. I wanted to be able to provide for him, give him a good life, a cultured life." She dabbed her eyes. "I couldn't bring him home where everyone would pressure me and Brooks to get married whether he wanted to or not."

Donna pushed her cup and saucer forward, leaned back, and asked, "Whether he wanted to or not? What did you want?"

170

"I wanted him to want me, not to feel obligated."

"He wants you now. Everyone can see that. And I think you still love him."

"Love and lust are not the same thing. I'm mature enough now to know the difference." The moisture in her eyes made the dust motes glitter in the sunlight streaming through the window.

Donna raised her eyebrows. "You and Brooks loved each other before you were old enough to know about lust."

Katie shook her head. "Childish puppy love is not real love."

"Oh? When it lasts from first grade through high school—I think it's the real deal. And let me tell you something. Love between a man and a woman would be pretty shallow without passion." She smiled. "After twenty-five years, when I look at your father, I still think he's the most handsome man I ever saw. My heartbeat races, I get all warm inside, and I still *lust* for him." She laughed. "I sure will be glad when I'm well enough to enjoy married life again."

"Mom! TMI—too much information!"

Donna laughed again. "I don't think so. Maybe we should have had this talk a long time ago." Katie stood, but her mother said, "Hear me out on this. In Genesis after the fall, God told Eve He would greatly increase her pain in childbirth, but even so, her desire would be for her husband, and he would rule over her." She smiled. "A good man, a loving man has power over a woman, over her heart, soul, and body. The key is to find a good man who feels the same way about you, marry him, and love him with all your being."

"And you think Brooks is that man?"

Donna shook her head. "Oh, not for me. My heart belongs to Richard Kane. I could never even look at another man the way I look at your father."

"You know what I mean." She shook her head. "Brooks is not that man for me, either. I have *looked* at other men, and he's done a lot more than just look at other women."

"In your *looking,* have you found one that makes your knees wobble, your belly flip-flop, and your heart beat ninety-to-nothing?"

"No, but I'm not finished looking."

"I do hope you'll find the right man, and I hope you'll know it when you see him."

Chapter Twenty-seven

"Dad, are you listening to me?" Austin tugged on his dad's arm.

"Sorry, Pardner. What were you saying?"

"I was talking about my daytime dream. When we get the big house, I want a cowboy room. I saw some stuff in a catalog Grandpa Richard had. My friend Cantu has a racecar bed and a racecar bedspread and all kinds of race car stuff. His parents are rich, so they live in a big house. But it's not bigger than our house is gonna be."

Brooks laid aside his tools and stooped to face his son. "Austin, it's ok to dream." He sighed. "It's good to dream, but sometimes our dreams don't come true." He paused, searching for the right words. "Look at this fence. Once it was a part of your Grandpa Richard's dream to have a fine ranch with lots of good cattle and a strong fence to hold them in. Over time, the poles get weak, and if you don't keep working on it, it will fall down and the cows will get out."

Austin looked confused. "What does that have to do with my dream?"

"Um, I don't know." He took his hat off and wiped the sweat from his brow. "I guess that wasn't a very good example." He turned his hat in his hand. "Well, it's kind of like that old bull your mom had. He was your mom's pet. Her dream was to keep him as a pet, but he grew up. He didn't want to stay on the Kane Ranch. He wanted to wander around, break down fences so he could meet other cows and fight with other bulls. They didn't want the same thing. You have a dream, but you can't force your dream on your mom when she wants something else."

"All my mom wants is to go to Chicago and play in the symphony."

"No, she's your mother and she loves you very much. She wants what's best for you, and if she thinks living in Chicago is best, then that's the way it will be." *At least for now.*

"No, I don't want to go!" Austin removed his hat, mimicking his father, and wiped his forehead. He looked deep into his father's eyes. "Do you want me and Mom to go back to Chicago?"

Oh, Lord. You know what I want, but I can't go against Katie, not in front of Austin. "I want your mom to be happy."

"What about me?"

"You were happy in Chicago with your mother. From now on, you'll have two places to be happy."

"Sometimes I was lonely. I'm never lonely here."

Brooks hugged his son. "I've been lonely, too. Now that we have each other, we won't be lonely anymore. We can talk on the phone every day, and we'll see each other a lot. I promise."

As Brooks mended the fence, he thought about Katie's reaction at breakfast. *Lord, I saw the revulsion on her face. Thinking about intimacy with me made her sick to her stomach. I thought there was hope for us. I thought she still loved me, but I guess I was dead wrong.*

Austin continued to talk about his dream house. His bedroom would have a horse bedspread with blue background, his brother would have one with green background, and his sister would have one with pink. "What kind of bedspread would you like for you and Mom?"

"Austin, we need to slow down. You show me that catalog, and I can order the bedspread you want for you, but we need to wait on the rest. There is no house or brother or sister."

Austin smiled. "Not yet, but there will be."

On the drive back to the house, Brooks sang, "One Day at a Time."

***

That evening, Brooks took his Bible and walked to the old oak tree. He texted Katie and asked her to call him after she put Austin to bed. He read and reread I Corinthians 13, a passage he and Katie memorized in high school when they were part of the True Love Waits

Campaign.

When she called, he said, "Katie I have some things to say, so please hear me out."

"I already told you not to say you love me."

"If I don't say I love you, will you listen to me?" When she didn't respond he took a deep breath and began his practiced speech. "In high school we memorized I Corinthians Chapter Thirteen, but memorizing scripture and applying it are two different things. Love is patient and kind, but I wasn't patient or kind when I was twenty and you were eighteen, and I'm sorry."

"Brooks . . ."

"Katie please let me finish. Love isn't self-seeking, but I was. I wanted to satisfy my desires regardless how it hurt you. Love isn't easily angered and keeps no record of wrongs. After you broke up with me, my anger simmered under the surface, ready to explode at the least provocation. Every time you entered my thoughts, I told myself how bad you were, when in reality I was the bad one."

"Brooks . . ."

"Please, Katie, let me finish, and then you can say whatever you want." He took another deep breath and continued, "Love always protects, but I didn't protect your innocence. Love always trusts, but I didn't trust you when you said you wanted to come home and get married. Again I was selfish, wanting what I wanted without thinking about you. I should have trusted your integrity and virtue when I found

176

out you were pregnant. I should have known the baby was mine." His voice broke. "Austin, our baby." He fought for composure. "Love always perseveres, but I didn't keep believing in you. I didn't hold on to what we had. Love never fails, but I failed you. Love always hopes," he took another deep breath, "and I hope that someday you can find it in your heart to forgive me."

After a pause, Katie asked, "Are you finished?"

"Yes."

"You're giving yourself way too much credit. I knew what was coming. The passion, like a crescendo, built with each passing year. I wanted to wait until we were married, but I didn't want to wait. I thought when you graduated and went on the road that things would cool down, but they didn't. Every time we were together, the desire surged to new heights." She paused, thinking about the morning's conversation with her mother. "I knew what was going to happen that night, because that's what I wanted. I just didn't plan on getting pregnant."

"Katie . . ."

"Don't interrupt." She sighed. "You didn't mention pride. I was proud of the way I could make you feel, and I delighted in the evil of leading you on and letting you down time and time again, until *I* couldn't wait any longer. I wasn't patient or kind, and I didn't protect your innocence, either." She took a deep breath and continued, "You've apologized to me, but I need to apologize to you. Just like

177

you said, you've always followed my lead. You did exactly what I wanted you to do, and then I blamed you for it. When I found out I was pregnant, I tried to manipulate you without telling you the truth. I became angry and blamed you for everything, when in reality I'm the guilty party."

"No, Katie, you are not to blame. I knew what was happening. I didn't stop because I didn't want to. I should have asked you to marry me as soon as you graduated. We could have eloped. A long distance relationship would have been difficult, but I think we could have made it."

"I don't think so. The green flecks in my hazel eyes reflect my jealous nature. You are so good-looking, add in your smooth voice, and women everywhere would be all over you. I wouldn't have been able to handle that."

"Katie, I've never loved anyone but you. You're the only girl, woman, I've ever wanted."

"You said you wouldn't say that."

"I didn't say those exact words." Even though she couldn't see him, he crossed his heart. "So what now? Where do we go from here?"

"I don't know." She paced the porch. "I'd like to start from the beginning, as friends, just friends. Give me some time and space. Let's try to practice the virtues we ignored six years ago."

"I'll try my best." He looked at the night sky, lit up with thousands of stars. *God you created the heavens and the earth. You knew me before you created me. If Katie is your plan for my life, please help me be patient and not ruin it.*

"Good night, Katie." He ended the call and whispered "I love you."

***

Wednesday evening Austin ate a hot dog instead of cabrito, because he *just couldn't* eat a baby goat. He enjoyed two helpings of chocolate cake and ice cream. Richard and Katie played their violins accompanying Brooks, Carmela, and Abuelo who played their guitars and sang. Austin played a solo of "Old McDonald" and "Jesus Loves Me" on his violin.

"Does anyone want anything else before a certain young man has to go to bed?"

"I do!" Austin ran in the house and returned with the catalog, showing his dad the bedspread he wanted. "Okay, Pardner. What size bed do you have?"

"Twin."

"Katie, what size curtains would fit his window?"

"I already have curtains."

Austin said, "When we get our big house, you can share a room with my dad instead of me, and you can pick out new curtains." Turning the page he said, "And this is the bedspread for my brother and this pink one is for the baby sister."

Thankful for the dim light, Katie felt the fire in her cheeks as every eye focused on her. "Austin, take the catalog to our room, and I'll look at the curtains later. And please, look in the closet and get my, my, um, my pink jacket."

When the door closed behind him, Katie stammered to explain, but Brooks intervened. "Austin is very bright and has a vivid imagination. He has dreamed up a house and a family. I'm trying to explain that it's good for everyone to have dreams, but we can't force our dreams on other people."

Silence hung heavy in the air, like the stillness in the eye of a tornado. Katie wished she could be picked up and carried away to the land of Oz. Nobody said anything until Austin banged through the screen door. "I couldn't find a pink jacket."

"Oh, I must have left it in Chicago."

Austin looked confused. "I don't remember a pink jacket? I thought you hate pink."

Abuelo said, "Maybe we need some pink. How about 'A White Sport Coat and a Pink Carnation'. "

When he finished the song, Donna said, "I think you sing that even better than Marty Robbins. Katie, would you close out our little party with something classical?"

Katie closed her eyes and played "Fir Elise" by Beethoven, losing herself and her embarrassment in the haunting melody.

After tucking Austin into bed, Katie said, "You know, Austin, when you make a wish before blowing out your birthday candles?"

He nodded.

"Well, some dreams are like wishes. If we tell what they are, they won't come true. Other dreams are like prayers; we just tell them to God. He hears all our prayers. Sometimes He answers yes. Sometimes He answers not yet, wait a while. Sometimes He answers no because He has something better for us. Sometimes He gives us new dreams, different dreams."

"How long do you think I'll have to wait for my dream?"

"I don't know." She kissed his forehead. "Close your eyes and sleep tight."

He smiled. "You forgot to say sweet dreams."

"Sweet dreams."

***

Thursday on the drive to Lubbock, Katie told her mother, "Our conversation the other day shocked me. I mean, I've never heard you talk like that, and I've hardly ever seen you and dad act affectionate to one another."

"We were both raised in conservative Christian homes. Our parents were never openly affectionate, and they certainly didn't talk about sex. Christians are people like everyone else. We don't have to put on a show for the world, but that doesn't mean we don't have feelings."

Katie kept her eyes on the road, so Donna continued. "God created woman to complete man, to be his helpmate, his companion.

181

Sex is a beautiful gift He gave to be shared between husband and wife. True love takes time to develop. Passion can come quickly and burn out, but with real love and commitment, it can last a life time. That's what I hope you'll find some day."

"With Brooks?"

"With the man God created especially for you, whoever that may be."

Katie drummed her fingers on the steering wheel. "Do you think there's only one man for one woman?"

"There is for me." Donna sighed. "I've known lots of people who fell in love and got married, but it didn't last. Maybe they lacked commitment. Maybe they didn't really know the person they married. Maybe one person betrayed the other's trust, and they couldn't forgive. For whatever reason, the marriage ended, but that wasn't the end of the world. God is always ready to forgive and give us another chance. We just have to ask for and accept His forgiveness."

"You heard Austin's dream last night. What am I going to do about that?"

"All children have dreams. The first time I went to a circus, I dreamed of being a trapeze artist. Since I'm afraid of heights, that dream didn't happen. I dreamed of being a singer, but I can't carry a tune in a bucket. Little boys dream of being policemen or firemen."

"Or cowboys."

Donna took a sip of her bottled water. "Country boys don't

dream of being cowboys. Most children dream of things far removed from their reality."

"Like me dreaming of playing in the Chicago Symphony."

"Once your Aunt LeAnn introduced you to the symphony, that wasn't out of the realm of possibility. God gave you natural ability and you have worked hard to develop that talent."

"Yes, but I still haven't achieved my goal."

"God only expects us to do our best and leave the results to Him."

***

While Donna received her IV chemo treatment, huddled beneath her prayer quilt, Katie searched the internet on her phone for positions as a music teacher. There were a few openings near Lubbock, but two hours each way would be too long to commute. Besides, she didn't have a Texas teaching certificate. She could complete the required courses on line but not before school started.

On the drive home, Katie relayed the results of her search. "So even if I wanted to stay, I couldn't because I couldn't get a job."

Donna had her seat reclined as far as it would go. She nodded her head and whispered. "I'll pray that God will show you what He wants you to do, what's best for you and Austin. Our home is your home. We may not have a lot, but what we have is yours. You can stay as long as you want." She closed her eyes. "I'm going to rest now."

As she drove home in silence, Katie prayed. *Dear Lord, Austin is my life, not Chicago, not symphony, but Austin. He's happy here. My parents aren't rich, and I wouldn't feel right mooching off them. Brooks wants to get married, but I'm scared to death. What if I gave up my job and my apartment, and it didn't work out? Where would I be then?* Her spirit felt as flat as the West Texas landscape.

Chapter Twenty-eight

By the time they arrived home, Donna was feeling the full effect of the chemo. Weak and nauseous, she said, "Katie, I don't feel like eating or smelling food. Do you think you could take Austin to Pat's and get him a hamburger or something?"

She washed her mother's face with a cool cloth. "Maybe Brooks can take him. I don't want to leave you."

"Once the anti-nausea medicine knocks me out, I'll sleep all evening. You've been working so hard, you deserve a night off."

Her dad rolled the wheelchair to the bedside. "You go on out, Katie. I'll stay here with your mother. If I feel like eating, I'll fix a sandwich out of the leftover cabrito."

"But, Dad, you're in a wheelchair."

"I'm not an invalid!" He cleared his throat. "I didn't mean to snap at you, but I am capable of taking care of myself and my wife."

She nodded. "Before I leave, can I get either of you anything?"

185

Her mother shook her head and her dad said, "Not right now."

Katie went into the kitchen and made a couple of sandwiches, placing them in Ziploc bags in the refrigerator. She filled the ice bucket and placed it on the table next to her dad's favorite mug where it would be easily accessible. She placed chips and cookies on the table. She brushed her teeth, touched up her makeup, and sat on the porch swing.

When Brooks and Austin pulled into the drive, she walked out to meet them. After explaining her mother's condition, she said, "I'm going to take Austin to Pat's for dinner. If you'd like to go with us, I could pick you up."

"I'd like to go, but only if I pick you up. My mama raised me to be a gentleman, and no way would I allow you to pick me up."

She smiled. "It's not a date."

Maybe not to you. "Just give me thirty minutes to clean up, and I'll be back to get you." He flashed her his sunshine in my soul smile.

She chuckled. "Okay. That will give Austin time to shower." She turned Austin toward the house. "Go get some clean clothes."

His face lit up. "Yes, ma'am."

Katie extended her hand to Brooks. "Friends, remember?"

He caressed her hand with his thumb. Looking into her eyes, he whispered in a husky voice, "Friends."

She watched him saunter to his pickup, covering the distance in a few graceful strides, the butterflies in her stomach in a flurry. *Just friends, that's all.*

Chapter Twenty-nine

Austin chatted all the way to town. After they ordered, Brooks got change so Austin could select some songs on the juke box. Half way through their meal, a leather-faced old rancher stopped by their table. "Brooks." He tipped his hat, "Katie. And this is your little boy?"

Katie could feel the blush and knew her face matched the red in her shirt. "Yes, this is my son. Austin, this is Mr. Jameson."

"Hello, Mr. Jameson." Austin patted Brooks on the shoulder. "And this is my dad."

Mr. Jameson nodded. "Uh-huh, I see that. Katie how's your mom?"

"She's doing much better. She had her last chemo treatment today in Lubbock. She's home resting now. With my dad."

"I heard about his accident. How's he getting along?"

"He should be up and around in a couple more weeks. Brooks has been taking care of things at the ranch." She tried to sit still and not squirm beneath the crusty old man's stare.

A sly smile slid across Mr. Jameson's face. "I bet he has."

Brooks started to stand, but Katie stretched her leg under the table and nudged him. She reached across the table and took his hand. He wrapped his large hand around hers and said, "Mr. Jameson, I don't remember you ever going to church before, but I'd like to invite you to the cowboy church."

"I heard you were singing in their band. A big step down from the big time, ain't it?"

Brooks met his gaze and held it. Then he said in his slow, southern drawl, "Actually, sir, I think serving God is a huge step up. I've never been happier."

"I never had much use for church and the hypocrites in it." Mr. Jameson scowled. "You planning to stay around?"

Brooks caressed Katie's hand with his thumb, the callous sending tingles up her arm. "Yes, sir, I'm home for good."

"So ya'll going to get married, *finally?*"

"My, you are quite inquisitive considering we haven't seen you for six years, and you never were all that friendly." Katie could feel the fire flaming through her eyes. "Unless you consider your crude flirtations friendly, which I never did. I don't think your wife did either. How is she by the way?"

The front door of the café opened, and Deputy Smith walked in. Brooks stood and met the deputy half way across the room. Giving his friend a bear hug, he whispered, "Can you get that old man out of here before I knock him flat?"

They walked to the table together. "Hey, Katie, Austin." Turning to the old man, Smith said, "Henry, how's your wife? I haven't seen her for a while. Maybe I'll just go out to your place and see if she's fallen down any more stairs."

"No need to come nosing around. I'm on my way to see about her now." Mr. Jameson strutted to the front door like a bantam rooster.

"That has to be the meanest snake that ever lived. His wife has had a broken arm and multiple bruises just since I've been on the force. Who knows what that poor woman puts up with or why she won't press charges." Brandon Smith shook his head. "The daughter lives in Dallas. She calls every once in a while asking us to go out and check on her mom."

"You think he beats his wife?" Katie asked. "I never liked him, but I didn't know he was that bad."

"I'm sure of it but nothing we can do as long as she makes up stories about falling down the stairs and tripping over the chickens."

"My mom and dad are going to get married, *finally*. Mr. Jameson said so." Austin beamed.

Brandon slapped Brooks on the shoulder. "Glad to hear it, man!" He leaned over and hugged Katie. "Congratulations. I always knew you two were meant to be together."

Katie pulled away from Brandon and looked at her son.

"Austin, Mr. Jameson *asked* if we were getting married. We didn't say we're getting married."

The little boy scooted out of the booth and hugged his dad around the legs. "But I know you are. It's my dream, and I've been praying about it."

Brandon laughed. "Well, there you go. Out of the mouths of Babes."

"Austin, remember our discussion last night? Somethings we don't talk about, like wishes, or they won't come true." *God, look at that face. He's so happy. Please don't let him get his little heart broken.*

Brandon smiled. "My lips are sealed. Your secret is safe with me."

"Thanks man." Brooks turned Austin back toward the booth. "Finish eating your dinner so we can go for a ride. You can take your milkshake with you."

Katie sat in the booth while her stomach bounced around the world and back. Brooks dug into his chicken fried steak, unfazed by the chaos of the evening. Austin slurped his milkshake, and she couldn't keep from laughing.

Austin laughed, too. "This is the best chocolate shake ever."

"Finish your hamburger. Remember, a man needs protein." Brooks winked at his son.

Katie picked at her fried okra. She couldn't get that when she

191

went back to Chicago, if she went back to Chicago.

When they left Pat's, Brooks turned north instead of south.

"Where are we going?" Katie asked.

"I have something to show you, so just relax and enjoy the ride."

Brooks pulled off the highway onto a dirt road. He stopped at an old metal gate, got out of the pickup, and unlocked the padlock. He continued to drive until he came to an old ranch house surrounded with trees.

He got out and hurried around to open the door for Katie. He helped her and Austin down, continuing to hold their hands as he led them to the front porch.

"Who lives here?" Katie asked looking around at the unkempt yard.

"Nobody right now." Using a key, he opened the front door. "Do you remember the Vaughns? Their kids were older than us, but my grandfathers were friends with Mr. Vaughn."

Stepping inside, Katie looked around. The décor screamed 70's with the green, orange, and gold floral print sofa and shag carpet. The musty smell assaulted her senses. Outlines on the walls showed where the china cabinet used to sit, where pictures once hung. Dust covered the harvest gold appliances in the kitchen.

"Mr. Vaughn was in a nursing home, so it's been empty for quite a while. The kids said he never changed anything after his wife died, and his heirs couldn't sell the place until he passed."

Katie looked searchingly at Brooks. *What is he talking about?*

"The land is good and fertile. The barn is actually in better condition than the house."

"And?" *God, please don't tell me what I think he's saying.*

"I've been looking for some land. Even though there's not much ranch property on the market, I got this at a great price."

"You bought this place?" Katie looked around the house in disbelief.

"I bought it for the land. I want to build and expand my family's business, do some marketing, PR publicity." He looked desperate. "My family raises the best cutting and roping horses anywhere. I'd like to promote them across the country, maybe internationally. I bought a new stud and mares to expand our breeding stock. My dad can never rodeo again, but watching him with Austin, I'd like to help him set up roping clinics. He is a world champion roper—young kids dream of being like him. I'd like to increase our legacy for my son. For our son."

"So, you're going to live here?" Katie asked.

"Is this our house?" Austin asked.

"This is my house, Austin." He hugged his son. Looking at Katie, he said, "I saved and made some good investments. The property is mine free and clear. The house needs a lot of work before it's livable. I have enough money left for some remodeling. In time I could add on or eventually build a new house."

"It doesn't have a big porch all around." Disappointment showed on Austin's face.

"Not yet, Son. Maybe you can help me build one when you come to visit."

"I won't live here with you?" His lip quivered.

"Yes, when you're here you'll live with me."

Katie turned and walked back through the living room, into the short hall leading to three small bedrooms and one old, outdated bathroom.

"The very first thing I plan to do is knock this wall out and make one bedroom out of these two. I was thinking of putting a master bathroom along this entire wall with a wraparound closet behind it. The next thing would be the kitchen—well, actually I'd probably do both of those things at the same time."

Katie tried to capture his vision. "Does your family know about this?"

"Of course. After I looked at it, I asked Gramps and Abuelo for their input, mostly about the land, but also the house." He searched her face, as though trying to read her thoughts. "My family built the house we live in. Between my dad and grandfathers, they can do about everything." He walked into the other bedroom. "Austin this will be your room, with the blue cowboy bedspread and curtains. Abuelo is a master wood-worker. He built a cowboy bed with a real wagon wheel headboard and footboard when I was a boy. I got too tall for it, but he's saved it all these years to give to my son, which is you."

"What about the bedrooms for my brother and sister?"

"This is just temporary, for a few years. Then I'll add on or build a new house."

"It's getting dark. We better head home," Katie said, turning toward the front door.

"Austin, maybe tomorrow we can come back and I'll show you the barn and the pastures. One for horses and one for cattle. Mighty Fine can be the start of your own herd." As they walked out on the porch, Brooks said, "Even though this porch doesn't go all the way around, we still have room for a porch swing and a couple of rockers."

The little boy smiled and held his dad's hand.

Back on the highway, Brooks said, "Beautiful night, isn't it? Just look at all those stars."

"I never knew there were so many stars till I came to Texas," Austin said. "In Chicago the lights and the tall buildings hide the stars."

"I know what you mean. This is one of the things I missed most when I was on the road." Brooks looked across his son's head and winked at Katie. "Just one of the many things I missed." Austin yawned. "Hey little man, lean your head on my shoulder and rest for a while."

He fell asleep and Brooks carried him into the house, waiting until Katie took his boots and jeans off and tucked him. "Will you sit with me on the porch a while?"

Katie sat in one of the rockers instead of the swing. "I am overwhelmed. I don't know what to say about what happened at Pat's . . . and the house."

Brooks pulled the other rocker close to her. "Jameson is a jerk, but I'm afraid other people are wagging their tongues about Austin, and about us—one of the drawbacks of a small town."

She nodded, staring up at the stars. *That wasn't a problem in Chicago. Nobody knew your business because nobody cared.*

"The property has been in the works for weeks. I just closed the deal yesterday while you were in Lubbock."

"I thought we agreed to take it slow and start with being friends again." Katie couldn't look at him. She didn't want to hurt him, didn't want to let him down *or* get his hopes up. She didn't know what she wanted.

"Love is patient. I'm willing to wait. I can live in the apartment above the barn while I remodel the house."

"I have to decide in the next two weeks if I'm going to sign my teaching contract for next year." Her voice sounded tired.

"You didn't already sign it?" His voice was barely above a whisper.

"No. Private schools are different than public schools. They wait until they do reviews and parent evaluations. They look at enrollment and budget, which varies each year. They offered me the contract two weeks ago, but I haven't signed it." He was invading her space, so she stood and walked to the railing. With her back turned to him, she said, "I've checked, and the only positions for music teachers are in Lubbock. I can complete the teaching requirements on line, but not before school starts."

He walked up behind her, not touching her, but she could feel his breath on her hair, smell his manly cologne. In a husky voice he said, "I could take care of you, Katie. You could work if you wanted, but you wouldn't have to. And I'm not like Jameson. I'd never hurt you."

She shook her head. "Please don't say anything else. My head is spinning."

He stepped back. "Okay. Good night, Katie. Sleep tight and have sweet dreams." He stepped off the porch and walked to his pickup. He didn't look back or turn back and wave.

She watched him drive away before she went into the barn to feed Mighty Fine. "I know you're hungry, you poor little orphan." How sad the baby's mother died giving birth, but he would survive. She thought about Austin, not knowing his dad, not experiencing a complete family, until now. Would he survive if Katie took him back to Chicago? Yes, he would survive, but he would be sad, to give up his dream, to be without his dad. She would be sad if she gave up her dream. *But sometimes God gives us new dreams, better dreams. Yes,*

Mom, I do believe you're right.

***

Brooks drove back to the old house, his property, and sat on the porch looking at the stars, listening to the crickets, the frogs, the Texas wind blowing through the trees. *Well, Lord, I hadn't planned on things happening like this. Henry Jameson, that old snake, got my blood boiling. He has no tact. I want to protect Katie and Austin from people like him. I want us to be a family. Maybe I should have looked for something closer to Lubbock, but then the prices would have been higher, out of my reach. It will be easier to build the business if I'm close, and the extra pasture land will help, too.*

Brooks unlocked the door and went inside. No, it doesn't look like much now, but it could be something special, a cozy, comfortable home. Without Katie and Austin, it would only be an empty, old house.

He walked out to the pickup and got the sledge hammer. He carried it into the first bedroom and began knocking holes in the adjoining wall. Each swing created more debris, more mess. *Like my life. A time to tear down and a time to build up. A time to gain and a time to lose. Lord, I hope this is the right time, the time to love not hate.*

He thought about Joshua and the Battle of Jericho. The Israelites were up against a powerful enemy. God told Joshua to cross the Jordan River at flood stage. When they took that first step of faith, the waters stopped flowing from upstream and stood in a heap. Then they walked across on dry land. God instructed the army to march around the city of Jericho, blowing their trumpets, once a day for six days. *Lord, Katie and I have been apart for six years.* On the seventh day, the army marched around seven times. At the sound of the trumpet blast, the people shouted for the Lord, and the walls came tumbling down. *Lord, there's a wall between Katie and me. I can't knock it down. I'm calling on Your mercy and power to perform a mighty miracle and break down the barrier between us.*

When he finished knocking down the wall, he felt bone tired. "You're right, Abuelo, a good lather is good for man and beast. Maybe tonight I'll get a good night's sleep." On the drive home he sang, "Joshua Fought the Battle of Jericho, and the walls came tumbling down."

Chapter Thirty

Austin talked non-stop all through breakfast telling his grandparents about the house, how he and his dad were going to build a big porch all the way around, and how Mighty Fine would be the start of his own cattle herd.

"He's a fine bull. With a few healthy heifers, you should have a good herd in a few years," Richard told his grandson. He caught Katie checking the clock. "Your dad's a little late this morning. Did you keep him out too late last night?"

Austin giggled. "I don't know 'cuz I fell asleep." He jumped up when he heard the pickup pull into the drive. "There he is now."

Katie stopped him before he escaped. "No, sir, not until you wash your face and hands and brush your teeth." He ran to the restroom and back in a flash. When the screen door slammed behind him, Katie walked to the porch. Brooks lifted Austin and swung him off the first step.

"Brooks, did you eat breakfast?"

He turned and tipped his hat. "Yes, ma'am. Mom made egg and chili burritos." He walked to the pickup without looking back. Katie stood at the rail watching him drive away with her son. *With his son, our son.*

Her parents lingered at the table. As she cleared the dishes, she felt their stares, but neither of them said a word. Richard rolled his wheelchair to the counter and poured himself another cup of coffee. "Donna, would you like some more tea?"

"Yes, I do believe I would."

Katie felt her parents scrutinizing stares as she finished washing the dishes. "What?"

Her father raised his eyebrows. Her mother sipped her tea.

Katie wiped the counter top, again. "You might as well come out with it."

"What?" her father asked. Her mother began giggling.

"It isn't funny." Katie scowled.

"What's not funny?" Her father asked, sending her mother into a fit of laughter.

"So when did you know about the house?" Katie put her hands on her hips.

Richard took a gulp of coffee. "Brooks told me yesterday he bought the old Vaughn place so he could help expand his family's business."

"What did he tell you about the house?" Her mother continued to chuckle. "Mom, what is so funny?"

"I'm sorry, Katie. It must be the aftereffects of the anti-nausea medicine. Drugs do this to me sometimes," Donna said through her giggles.

Concern creased Richard's brow. "Maybe you need to go back to bed and rest."

She wiped her eyes with her napkin. "Katie, do you want to talk about it?"

"About Brooks's house? The one with the harvest gold appliances, the orange and green flowered sofa, the gold *shag* carpet, and the rusty tub?"

Through fits of laughter Donna said, "Everybody had those colors . . . in the 70's . . . like the mauve and blue of the 80's and 90's."

"Well, it doesn't concern me, because it's not my house."

"That little boy sure was excited," Richard said, his serious tone putting a damper on Donna's laughter.

Katie shook her head. "Yes, just like the puppy and the horses and the bull. How can I compete with that?"

"Like I always say, competition is for Four-H and fairs, not families." Her mother stood. "I believe I will go lie down." Richard followed her to their bedroom.

***

At 11:30 Katie called Brooks. "Can you and Austin come in for lunch? I made chicken and dumplings."

"I brought egg burritos for lunch. I want to work a little longer before I take Austin to see the place." When she didn't respond, he said, "I hope you don't mind. He has his heart set on it."

"Sure, that's fine." She paused. "Will you be back for supper?"

"Gramps, Abuelo, and I are taking the old furniture and appliances to Lubbock to donate to the mission. What they don't want, we'll take to the dump. I thought Austin could ride with us, and we could eat at the Cattleman's Steak House. Kind of a man's night out."

"Oh . . . okay. You will have him home by bedtime won't you?"

"Yes, Ma'am. Goodbye."

What is all this Ma'am stuff? And a man's night out with a child?

When her parents came to the table for lunch, she told them about the man's night out. Her father nodded. "A couple more weeks and I should be good as new. Then Brooks can spend all the time he needs on his own place."

"He'll need lots of time." Katie waved her hands. "Have you seen the house?"

"Before he went into the nursing home, Mr. Vaughn kept the place up, even if it was outdated," her mother added.

"It's good fertile land, especially since it's been fallow. Has a good barn, too." Richard took a bite of the chicken and dumplings. "Thank you, Katie, for fixing my favorite. Nothing at the Cattleman's Steak House could beat this."

***

The next day, Brooks didn't come in the house. He checked on the cattle and then took Austin to "their" house. Sunday he asked if he could take Austin after church to spend the day with his family. The day dragged on. Katie had just finished feeding Mighty Fine when Brooks pulled into the drive at 9:00. "Austin, go in and get ready for a shower. I'll be there in a few minutes."

Brooks hugged his son and turned toward his truck.

"Wait, I think we need to talk," Katie said closing the gap between them.

He took off his hat. "Ok, go ahead."

"I've hardly seen my son the past few days, and he should be in bed before 9:00."

Brooks looked at his watch. "I'm sorry. I guess I lost track of time. I'll do better tomorrow." He got in the truck.

"Wait." He looked at her without responding. She moved closer. "What are you trying to do?"

"What do you mean?"

"You know what I mean." Her hand went automatically to her hip. She dropped it so she wouldn't look combative.

"I've been working on my house, and I want to spend as much

time as possible with my son before you take him back to Chicago."

She fought tears. "I told you I haven't decided if I'm going back."

"No, ma'am, you said you haven't signed your contract." He ran his fingers through his thick wavy hair—she had an overwhelming urge to do the same thing. "I'm trying to give you your space, like you said."

"I said I wanted to be friends." She bit her lip to keep from crying. "Friends talk to each other."

He got out of the pickup and stood in front of her. "Go ahead and talk. I'm listening."

She took a step back, then stepped forward, ran her fingers through his hair, pulled his head down and kissed him. He pulled back. "What are you saying, Katie?"

"I've missed you," she whispered and kissed him again. Time slipped away. It seemed like an instant, like eternity, before he stopped and broke free of her embrace.

"You want to come to the house with us tomorrow?" His voice sounded breathless.

"I'd like that," she whispered. She tried to kiss him again, but he backed up.

"Good night, Katie." She watched him drive away, without looking back. *Okay, God, I don't know why I did that, but now he knows how I really feel about him. I guess we both know.*

***

Brooks felt the heat on his lips. *I'm speechless, God. I'm afraid to get my hopes up, but if that kiss is any indication, Katie's feelings for me are as strong as mine are for her. I'm putting my hope and trust in You. I'm asking for a miracle.*

Chapter Thirty-one

Monday morning Brooks waltzed up the walk whistling "I'm Leaving it All Up to You."

Austin opened the door before he could knock. "Come in, Dad. I'm almost finished with breakfast."

Katie's eyes met his, and she blushed.

Brooks appraised her from head to toe. Everything about her was perfect. He loved every inch of her. He wanted to take her in his arms and kiss her, but he couldn't take any liberties. Did the blush indicate regret about what happened last night? She held the reins of his heart, so he would follow her lead.

She opened the cupboard. "Would you like a cup of coffee?" her voice soft, tentative.

"No, thanks. It's already hot outside." Just being near her warmed his heart, raised his temperature higher than the thermometer. The happiness he felt bubbled over into a smile. "I'm going to make a quick check of the stock. If everything is okay, I want to spend the day working on my house." He twirled the hat in his hands. "My mom made bacon sandwiches, so we could have a picnic." He looked at the floor, then met her eyes. "There's enough if you want to come with us."

Austin bounced up and down. "A picnic! Mom, can you come?"

She smiled at her son. "I'd like that." Glancing at Brooks, she asked, "What can I make for our picnic?"

"Besides the sandwiches, Mom packed some cantaloupe and cookies. If you want to bring something else you can, but you don't have to."

"Will we be back in time for supper?"

"I can bring you back. Today's agenda is to tear out the kitchen cabinets, so I'd like to work until it's done."

"What if I fry some chicken for supper?"

Brooks shifted his feet. "I hate for you to go to that much trouble. Some more sandwiches would be fine."

"No trouble. I need to fix dinner for my parents anyway."

"Don't worry about us. We can make do." Donna stood and began clearing the breakfast dishes.

"We cleaned the apartment above the barn. It has a table and chairs, a refrigerator and stove that work. We could eat in there or at least store the food." Brooks put his arm around Austin. "Let's go,

Pardner. The sooner we get started, the sooner we can finish." He stopped at the door, his eyes appraising Katie's tank top and shorts. "You'll probably want to change clothes. Put on something old. Long pants and a long-sleeved shirt." His eyes followed her shapely legs down to her flip-flops and painted toenails. "Old boots, or at least shoes that protect your feet." *Nope, I couldn't get much work done with her looking like that.*

***

Katie ran water in the sink to wash the skillet and biscuit pan. Donna rummaged in the pantry and took some sliced ham out of the freezer. "Dad and I can eat ham sandwiches today. There's enough in this package for the three of you, too."

"Would you all like some cornbread salad? I think I'd like to make some now that I have your recipe. Maybe some deviled eggs?" She opened the refrigerator, studying the contents. She turned to find her parents watching her. "Is there anything you'd like me to make for you before I go? Anything you've been craving?"

"You've done a fine job taking care of us. Sandwiches will be fine." Donna got the cornmeal out of the pantry. "Do you want to make the cornbread, or do you want me to do it?"

"I'd like to do it all. Why don't you go on and rest for a while?"

Donna kissed her daughter on the cheek. "I think I will sit in my recliner and crochet."

Richard poured himself another cup of coffee and stayed in the kitchen. Katie mixed up the cornbread, pretending he wasn't in the room. "I'm going out to pick the garden. There should be some fresh tomatoes and onions for the salad. Tomorrow I'll fry up some okra. I promise." Her father nodded without saying anything.

She loved working in the garden, always had. In Chicago she grew tomatoes and herbs on her little patio. Someday, when she got her own house, she wanted to have flowers and roses all around the house with a big vegetable garden nearby.

***

Katie just finished feeding Mighty Fine when Brooks and Austin pulled into the driveway. He looked at her from head to toe. "Are you coming with us?"

"Yes. I didn't want to put on long clothes until I had to. I bet this is the hottest day we've had this summer." She couldn't read his expression. Was he mad? "It'll just take me a minute to change."

He nodded and walked over and started petting the baby bull.

Katie returned with her arms loaded down with food. He opened the back door, and took her bundles, helping her into the front seat. Austin talked about the picnics they had at the park in Chicago, feeding the ducks, watching the people. "Dad, do you think we can teach Poppy to catch a Frisbee?"

"Poppy?" Katie looked from Austin to Brooks.

"Yes. I picked my puppy and named him Poppy because he

hops around all the time. I don't think Hoppy is a good name because it sounds like a rabbit, so I named him Poppy, and his dad's name is Peppy." He looked up at his mother with wide-eyed innocence. "Do you think Poppy is a good name?"

"Yes, I think that is a great name." She forced a smile to hide her frown.

"Dad said he can come and live at our house when we move in."

Brooks kept his eyes focused on the road not offering any comment. She felt irritated that he had allowed Austin to pick out a puppy and name it. He couldn't have it in their apartment. That would break his heart if she went back to Chicago. *If is a big word.*

***

Katie was amazed at the progress Brooks had made in a few short days. The gold shag carpet had been ripped out exposing original hardwood floors. She bent down and ran her hands across the smooth surface of the wood. "Can this be restored?"

"Yes, Abuelo said he can replace a few boards, fill in the holes where the carpet strip was, sand and refinish it."

"I love hardwood." Katie felt the warmth of the wood seep into her being.

She walked into the first bedroom. "Wow! I can't believe what a difference this made just knocking down that wall." She walked around the room several times. "If you put a walk-around closet

behind a master bath, it would really cut into the size of the bedroom."
She paced off the space at the end of the room. "What if you put a
small walk-in closet on this side and just a regular bathroom over
here?"

He stared, mouth agape. "I could do that."

She walked to the middle of the room. "You could put the bed
here between the windows." *Get away from those thoughts.* She
moved to the end of the room. "You could put a dresser here and a
chest of drawers or armoire-TV cabinet there. I don't watch much
television, mostly cooking, gardening, remodeling, and redecorating
shows. *Fixer-Upper* with Chip and Joanna Gaines is my very
favorite."

"I like that show, too. Good down-to-earth Texans."

She walked into the old bathroom. "How hard would it be to
replace the tub? I don't know if that rust could come off."

"I plan on gutting this bathroom, all new everything."

She inspected every inch of the bathroom and then went to the
next bedroom. "So, Austin, this will be your room?"

"Yes, ma'am. I'm going to have my dad's old bed that Abuelo
built for him."

"The one with the wagon wheel?" He smiled and nodded. "I
remember it. That will look so good with your cowboy bedspread."
Austin hugged his mom.

Katie eyed the kitchen. "So you're going to tear out the

cabinets today?"

"That's the plan," Brooks said following her into the dining area.

She walked in circles, looking from floor to ceiling. "What would be the possibility of tearing out this wall, opening up the kitchen on either side of the door? If the cabinets could come out this far, you could put an island here with bar stool seating. You can tell they had a china cabinet there, probably a table in the center of the room, but with a big bar, you wouldn't need a table. That would create an open area with more living space."

Brooks looked at the wall. "I think that's doable. Let's go out back and eat our lunch." He led them to the back door. An old picnic table sat in a clearing surrounded by trees.

Austin ran to the tire swing in the big tree. "Don't get on that! The rope might be rotten," Katie yelled.

She moved toward him, but Brooks reached out and took her hand. "It's ok. We just put it up yesterday."

Birds fluttered in the trees singing their sweet songs as Brooks spread a red vinyl tablecloth on the table and removed the contents of the basket his mother had packed. "Would you like to swing, Katie? I could push you." The devilment danced in his deep blue eyes.

"So you can turn me around and around until I get sick?" She shook her head. "I don't think so."

He laughed. "That was pretty funny swinging you till you

puked."

"I didn't think there was anything funny about it." She shook her finger at him. "It wasn't funny on your Senior trip to Six Flags either, when you talked me into riding the Judge Roy Scream, and I barely got off before I barfed."

"You were the talk of the trip." His eyes searched her face, sending electrical currents through her body. "You were pretty much the talk of the school, being the prettiest, best dressed girl."

She smiled and winked. "Not to mention having the finest, most talented boyfriend." She looked at his full lips, wanting him to kiss her. The thought of him kissing her made her heart beat double time. But he didn't.

"Come push me, Dad." Brooks pushed his son, slowly, in a straight line. Austin giggled. *Lord, he is so happy here. He loves his dad. His dad loves him . . . And I love them both.*

"That's enough, Austin. We better eat so we can get to work."

When they finished eating, Brooks and Austin took Katie to the apartment above the barn so she could put their supper in the refrigerator. She appraised the living area, the bedroom, the bathroom. "Wow, this is nicer than the house."

"It's newer. Old Mr. Vaughn built it for his grandson, who lived in it for a couple years while going to Tech. Then he used it for hired help when he couldn't take care of the place alone."

They heard a pickup pull into the drive. Abuelo, Gramps, and

Dustin met them when they came out of the barn. "We came to help tear out that kitchen. It'll be a lot quicker with all of us," Gramps said to Brooks.

Abuelo handed Austin the puppy. Peppy jumped out of the back of the truck. "I thought Poppy could keep you company while we work, and Peppy will protect you both."

"Mom, this is Poppy. Isn't he pretty?"

She knelt and focused on the dog, averting the questioning glances of the three men.

While the men worked tearing out the cabinets, Katie watched Austin playing with the puppy. She swung in the tire, feeling the warmth on her face, the gentle breeze blowing her hair, and she prayed. *Lord, please give me wisdom to know what to do. Should I go back to Chicago? Should I stay here for Austin? What about what I want? What do I want?*

***

With the demolition of the kitchen complete, the older men left. Brooks took Katie by the hand and led her inside. "You were right. Tearing out this wall makes this living area seem twice as big. Tomorrow we're going to tear out the old bathroom." He led her to the open bedroom, the master bedroom. "Abuelo said it should be easy to put in the new bathroom if we align the plumbing adjacent to the other one. The closet would be on this side." He paused and looked at her. "So what do you think? We could put in a whirlpool tub, which would make the closet smaller, or we could put in a regular tub and have a bigger closet."

We? Katie raised her eyebrows. "Would *you* like a whirlpool tub?"

He blushed and looked away. "Well, not for me."

She turned to hide her smile. "If you plan to build on later, like a bigger master bedroom and bath, it would probably be better to just put a regular tub in here." She walked out of the room, looked at the old bathroom, and then into the smaller bedroom. "What about a Jack and Jill bathroom? If you could open this wall, Austin could have his own toilet, sink, and vanity. Then you could put one bathtub and shower in the middle, and another toilet, sink, and vanity open to the other bedroom. It would be great for kids." She felt the blush creep up her neck and flood her face thinking of Austin's daytime dream. "I mean, in case you have other kids . . . later on."

He retraced their steps back to the big bedroom. "I think I would rather have two full baths. In case there are other kids . . . later on. Growing up, it was a pain for the three of us kids to share a bathroom. I had to get up before the girls, or I couldn't even get in to take a shower." He walked to the living room. "I think I would like to add the master bedroom and bath off this wall, maybe build a patio under those trees, to watch the sun come up." He blushed again. "I mean . . . later on."

She walked outside, paced off the space to the trees. "I think that would be lovely." She picked up a fallen tree branch and drew lines in the dirt. "The porch could extend across the front of the house and along the side to a little courtyard right here." She walked around to the back yard. "What about another courtyard or patio here, off the kitchen?" She turned in circles. "We could drink coffee and watch the sun come up." She stuttered, "I . . . I, uh, mean . . . you could."

"And we could watch Austin swing." He didn't stutter.

She walked toward the barn. "Let's go wash up so we can eat."

Chapter Thirty-two

On Tuesday, Brooks worked past lunch. "Today we're going to tear out the old bathroom and get ready for the new one. It'll be a dusty, dirty job. Austin, I think you should stay here with your mom and grandparents."

"Aww, Dad." Brooks raised his eyebrows. Austin lowered his eyes and said, "Yes, sir."

Richard said, "I've been missing you, little man. How about a game of dominoes? The winner gets a double scoop of ice cream."

Austin smiled. "Okay."

A few minutes after he drove away, Brooks called Katie. "Would you like to go to Lubbock tomorrow and help me pick out new cabinets and appliances?" He paused, waiting for a reply. "Since you watch *Fixer Upper,* you probably have some good ideas about the kitchen. No pressure, no strings, just a friend helping a friend."

"I'd like that." She let out her breath. "Austin too?"

218

"Of course. It will be his house." When the call ended, he said, "I hope it will be your house, too, Katie . . . our house." He crossed his fingers, crossed his heart, closed his hands in prayer, looked up to heaven and said, "Please, Lord, let it be."

After tucking Austin in bed that evening, Katie sat on the front porch, surfing the internet on her phone. She bookmarked some kitchen cabinets, backsplashes, and countertops she liked.

***

The drive to Lubbock passed quickly with Brooks, Katie, and Austin singing silly songs, laughter filling the cab of the pickup. When they sang "I've Got the Joy," Katie felt indescribable joy. "And I'm so happy, So very happy," *Lord, it's true. Austin's never been happier. I've never been happier. I wish, I wish I could have peace knowing this would last, the peace that passes understanding.*

Katie shared her ideas for the kitchen. "I like white cabinets because they're bright and clean looking. I found this vintage backsplash that looks like the ceiling tiles in our county court house, only silver instead of white, which I think would add class and a bit of shine. It says they're easier to install than the glass tiles and much less expensive. These cabinets with the vertical groove pattern look like bead board, only not as pricy, adding a traditional country charm. This gray-ice quartz counter top would tie in the silver backsplash with the white cabinets. All the neutral colors would allow you to change and update accessories in any color."

He nodded. "I like that. What color accessories are you thinking?"

"It's your house, so that would be totally up to you."

He smiled. "Yes, but you're my decorator."

"Okay. I'm thinking red. I love the contrast of red and white. The hardwood floors and red accents would add warmth to the white and gray."

"Stainless steel appliances would look good with the white and silver."

"Oh, no." She felt the blush creep into her cheeks as soon as she blurted out her response. "I mean . . . it's your house . . . if that's what you want."

"If . . . if it was your house, what would you want?"

She averted his eyes. She couldn't look at him. She didn't want to get his hopes up. She didn't want to get her hopes up just to have them dashed. And they would be. Either her dreams of Chicago and symphony. Or building a home and a life with Brooks. Or Austin's dreams of a family. She sighed. "If . . . if it was my house, I wouldn't want stainless steel appliances. It's too industrial, like the school cafeteria I worked in at college." She shook her head. "Not pleasant memories."

He nodded. "So what color were you thinking?"

She giggled. "White of course. To go with the rest of the white . . . and red, or whatever color accessories you choose . . . for your house."

When they went into the large home improvement store, Katie showed the salesman what she had selected. Brooks gave the salesman the precise measurements, including where the sink and stove needed to be. The man configured the kitchen layout on his computer program, added everything up, and showed them the total. Katie's face paled. "Maybe we should look at simpler cabinets and laminate instead of quartz."

Brooks looked at the figures. "Deduct the installation of the cabinets and backsplash."

The salesman shook his head. "You don't want to spend this much money on cabinetry and take a chance on them not being installed correctly."

Brooks frowned. "My grandfathers are master craftsmen. I assure you they can do a better job hanging the cabinets than anyone you have working here. They could build the cabinets, but I don't want to wait that long. I want it done before school starts. Can you get them that quick?"

"Yes, I can have them in two weeks." The salesman refigured the amount. "This is what it would be without installation."

Brooks nodded. "Let's do it. Could you set up the installation of the countertop the next week?"

"That can be done. And how will you be financing?"

"I won't." He stood, pulling Katie by the hand. "Go ahead and take care of the paperwork while we look at appliances."

"Let me show you the appliances. Then I can order it all at once."

The salesman started to stand, but Brooks put his hand on his shoulder. "We can read the labels and decide without any help."

Brooks put his arm around Katie and led her toward the appliances. They stopped in front of the refrigerators. "Brooks, that is a lot of money. Are you sure you want to buy what I like?" She tried unsuccessfully to hold back the tears. "What if it doesn't work out?"

He lifted her chin, his violet blue eyes a wave of compassion. "I told you I wouldn't put any pressure on you. I like what you chose." He wiped the tears as they dripped down her cheeks. "I'm hoping and praying for a miracle, but if you don't choose me, I will have a nice house, something to remind me of your style and beauty." She put her arms around his waist and buried her face in his chest. He held her close, caressing her hair. "Please don't cry. It's going to be okay."

Austin stood in front of a refrigerator. "Look! This has the water and ice thing like the one my friend Cantu has. And see this drawer? I can get snacks out without opening the whole refrigerator and wasting electricity." He batted those long eyelashes. "That's what Cantu's mom says."

Katie looked at the tag. "Austin, we may need a plain refrigerator, like that one." She started to move away, but Brooks took hold of her hand and pulled her back.

"Austin, if this is the one you want, I think this is the one we should get." The little boy's frown turned into a smile.

Katie fingered the tag. "Brooks, it's so expensive."

"It's okay, I've got it covered. I think Austin should be able to choose something, and he will use the refrigerator." He laughed. "You can pick the dishwasher and stove."

"Because the woman cooks and does dishes?" She put her hand on her hip.

"Well, I'm sure you've done a whole lot more cooking and dishwashing than me. I'll choose the microwave. I can operate that, and everyone will have a say about something."

"But I chose everything else in the kitchen."

"Yes, but I chose the property . . . without talking to you." He pulled her close and whispered in her ear. "I want the house to be yours, if you want it."

She felt so warm and happy, so very happy deep down in her heart.

***

Austin wanted pizza for supper, followed by ice cream for dessert. He fell asleep on the way back to the ranch. Katie stared out the window in silence. "Brooks, if you want me, and I choose to stay, I don't have anything to add, no dowry, no money, nothing but a few pieces of furniture I picked up at thrift stores."

Brooks pulled off the highway, reached across the seat, and

pulled her face close to his. In a husky voice he said, "If you want me and choose to stay, that would make me the happiest man in the world." He kissed her, softly, tentatively. "You're worth more than rubies. More than anything in the world. More than the whole world." He kissed her long and deep, leaving her breathless before he pulled away and drove back onto the highway.

After a few minutes he said, "Celina's brother-in-law has a plumbing supply business. The next few days we'll be putting up the new walls and installing the plumbing and new fixtures in the bathrooms. I know you hate brown, so I've ordered light marbled-looking tiles. The colors will blend well with the kitchen colors you chose."

"You've always had an incredible memory." She smiled in the cover of darkness.

"I remember everything about you Katie." He cleared his throat. "I love everything about you."

Chapter Thirty-three

The next three days, Katie and Austin barely saw Brooks while he worked on the bathrooms. She invited both families for Sunday dinner and spent all day Saturday cooking lasagna, cannelloni Alfredo, and caramel cheesecake. She hoped Brooks would take her to see the house so they could have some time together, alone.

After dinner, the family sat on the front porch, Richard and Katie with their violins, Carmela and Abuelo with their guitars, singing songs, songs about home and family. Dustin asked Carmela to sing "500 Miles"—Katie thought how sad their life had been, him riding the rodeo circuit, winning buckles, making money, leaving his family behind, and ruining his health. Dean asked Abuelo to sing "Georgia" such a soulful melody, and she knew he must still miss his wife Georgia, who died when Dustin was a young boy. Brooks ended with Carrie Underwood's "Temporary Home" and Blake Shelton's "Home".

225

"Can we end with something happy, something upbeat?" Richard asked. Taking his wife's hand he said, "How about 'Forever and Ever, Amen'?"

Katie felt the blush flood her face when Brooks looked deeply into her eyes while singing the proclamation of undying love. *Lord, I hope it's true. I hope we can love each other for ever and ever. Amen.*

As the Travis family prepared to leave, Austin invited them to the barn to see his bull. Katie took Brooks by the hand and dawdled as the rest of the family hurried to keep up with the excited little boy. She looked into his eyes, giving him a demure smile. "When are you going to take me to the house so I can see what you've done?"

"In a couple more days it should be presentable." He arched his eyebrows. "I can get more work done without any distractions."

She bumped her hip against his. "So now I'm a distraction?"

He leaned over and whispered in her ear, "You better believe you are. Too much of a distraction."

His husky voice melted her resolve. "I've really missed you. A few kisses might be a good diversion." She licked her lips. "You know what they say about all work and no play."

He led her to the side of the barn, wrapped her in his arms, and kissed her passionately. When he pulled his lips away, he hugged her closer, caressing her back. His heart pounded in his chest, his uneven breathing rustled her hair. Finally he said, "I love you so much. I want to finish the house as quickly as possible so we can get married." He stroked her hair. "With every board I cut, every nail I pound, I think of you. I put my heart and soul into everything in that house, because I want it to be perfect for you, for Austin, for our family."

"I want to be part of the house. It will go faster if I help." She looked into his eyes, a sea of swirling passion, and she lost herself. She put her hands on the back of his neck and drew him close, kissing him with all the emotion she had kept buried for the past six years.

"Do you want to run away to Lubbock and get married tonight?" He moaned, "How many times did we almost elope when we were kids? Now we're actually old enough."

She stepped back. "On second thought, I don't think I should go to the house tonight. Tomorrow we're taking my dad to Lubbock to get his cast off." She sighed. "Do you want to keep Austin with you? I think he would like that."

He dropped his arms and ran his fingers through his hair. He took deep breaths, trying to steady his uneven breathing.

She turned around and took a step. "We better go inside. Everyone will be wondering where we are."

He took her hand and pulled her back. "Katie, don't kiss me like that again unless you're ready to get married."

Her legs wobbled, and she felt like she might faint. "I'm sorry. I didn't mean to."

"I meant everything I said, and my kiss was sincere." He released her hand and walked ahead of her into the barn.

Austin looked up as Mighty Fine finished off his bottle. Looking at his parents, he said, "Where were you?"

The adults scrutinized Katie and Brooks. Carmela blushed and said, "We need to go home." She hugged Austin and told him goodnight. Dustin followed his wife out of the barn. The grandfathers bragged on Mighty Fine and the good job Austin was doing taking care of him. Gramps said, "See you tomorrow, Brooks." He tipped his hat. "Katie."

"Austin, would you like to stay with me tomorrow or go with your mom and grandpa to the doctor in Lubbock?"

Austin hugged his dad. "I want to stay with you," he looked questioningly at his mother, "if it's okay."

"I think that would be a lot more fun than riding in the car and sitting in a waiting room. You haven't seen your dad much the past few days."

Austin hugged his mom. "Thank you!"

After tucking him in bed, Katie had trouble sleeping. She knew she loved Brooks. She had never been attracted to anyone else. Love is built on passion, intimacy, and commitment. The passion definitely existed. They had shared emotional intimacy long before they shared physical intimacy. Commitment was the question. Could she trust Brooks to stay in the country after he'd tasted fame and fortune? Could she trust him to be committed to her and only her, for life? Could she commit to him and give up her dream to play in the symphony?

***

While sitting in the orthopedic waiting room, Katie's phone rang. Caller ID showed the Chicago Symphony Administration Office. "Hello, this is Katie Kane."

She walked out into the hall and took the call. A member of the symphony had suffered a heart attack and passed away. The conductor invited her to audition for a full-time position. "I like your style, Katie. I've been impressed each time you've practiced and played with us. You may need some extra tutorials, but I'm willing to mentor you . . . privately."

Katie's heart reeled. Her life-long dream. She had worked so hard, waited so long. She couldn't say no. The audition was set for Thursday. When she hung up, she booked a flight for Wednesday and called her aunt.

LeAnn said, "I was excited when Geoffrey called, personally, and asked for your number. This is the chance of a life-time. Your dream come true."

"He said I might need some private tutoring."

"Hmm." LeAnn sighed. "We can talk about that later. I can't wait to see you."

Over lunch at the Texas Land and Cattle Company, Katie told her parents about her plans. Her father dropped his fork and stared at her. Her mother asked, "Have you talked to Brooks?"

"No." She shook her head, avoiding her father's piercing eyes.

"I'll tell him tonight."

Her dad almost choked on his steak. "You're just going to *tell* him?"

"Yes, of course I'm going to *tell* him. I wouldn't leave without telling him." She laid down her fork, facing him head on. "I'm not that bad."

"I thought you might discuss it with him, ask what he thought. Talk to Austin."

Donna patted her husband's hand. "Katie, we know this has been your dream, everything you've worked for." She wiped her mouth with her napkin. "I have been praying that God would work His will in a way that would be best for everyone." She took a drink of water. "Whatever you decide, we will support you. Won't we Richard?" She squeezed his hand.

"It's your life." He dabbed his eyes with his napkin. "You will always be our daughter. We don't want to lose you again . . . or our grandson."

Katie put her hand on her father's shoulder as she stood. "I love you both, always and forever."

On the quiet drive home, Katie tried to think of how to tell Brooks, what she would say, how he might react.

Chapter Thirty-four

When they returned to the ranch, Katie said, "Is it okay if I heat up leftovers for your dinner? I'd like to talk to Brooks, alone."

"That's not necessary. Now that I got my cast off and your mother is feeling better, we can take care of ourselves."

Katie raised her eyebrows. "Dad, you still have a walking cast, and the doctor said you need to take things easy for a while."

"Don't boss me around, and I'll try not to tell you what to do," the gruffness of his voice showed his displeasure.

Katie looked for back-up from her mother, but she shook her head.

"Well, I'll go on out and feed the horses and Mighty Fine. I need to stretch my legs, anyway." Katie walked out the door, letting the screen slam behind her. *He's so dang stubborn. I hope he'll still let Brooks help him. Lord, I hope Brooks will still want to help him.*

She stayed outside, watering the flowers and the garden, until

Brooks pulled into the driveway. Austin jumped out of the pickup and ran into her arms. "You should see my bathroom. It's so neat, and it's all mine." He looked up at his mother and smiled. "Your bathroom looks neat, too."

She ruffled his hair. "You must have worked really hard because you're one dirty little boy. I've already fed Mighty Fine, so go on in and take a shower."

After Austin disappeared in the house, Brooks said, "If you don't have anything started for dinner, I thought we could go to Pat's. Maybe your parents would feel like going, too."

"It's been a really long day. We're all tired, and there's plenty here to eat." She forced a smile. "Could I see the house while Austin's taking a shower?"

He raised his eyebrows. "Just you and me?"

She gave him a playful punch on the arm. "Not like that. I just want to see what you've done." She walked to the passenger door and got in the pickup before he could open her door.

As they pulled out of the drive, Brooks asked about their trip to Lubbock and the doctor visit. She avoided his eyes. "Dad's ankle has healed pretty well. He has a walking cast. The doctor said he needs to take things slow and easy, but you know how stubborn he can be."

He laughed. "Like someone else I know."

She forced a smile and looked out the window. When they arrived at the house, he led her straight to Austin's bathroom. Its white vanity, gray and white marbled counter top, floor and shower tiles looked fresh and clean, as pristine as a model home. The brushed nickel faucets and light fixtures sparkled like a new dime. She glanced in the mirror and caught his dancing eyes, his million dollar smile, and her heart deflated like a popped balloon. *Lord, I feel so conflicted. How am I going to do this?*

He took her by the hand and led her to his bathroom, *their* bathroom. The tiles and fixtures were the same, only it had a larger vanity with double sinks and mirrors. She looked at the tub and imagined soaking in bubbles up to her chin. Trying to blink away the image, she focused on the mirror and saw his handsome face. She imagined washing off her makeup, while he watched her from their bed. Heat coursed through her body. She felt red hot, like she'd spent hours in the West Texas sun burning to a crisp. He took her hand and led her to the closet.

"I know this isn't a very big closet, but we could use the closet in the apartment to store our off-season clothes, just until we build a real master bedroom and bath with a big walk-in closet." He wrapped his arms around her and kissed the top of her head. He kissed her ears and whispered, "I can hardly wait until we're married."

She pulled away. "Can we go outside? It's kind of stuffy in here." *I'm so hot, I have to get out of this bedroom.*

Katie sat at the picnic table. Brooks started to sit beside her, but she motioned for him to sit on the opposite side. She held his hands, looked into his deep violet eyes, and cleared her voice. "Brooks, I think I fell in love with you in first grade. The first time I looked into your beautiful eyes." He smiled and leaned across the table to kiss her. She pulled away before losing her resolve. "Please let me finish." She blinked, fighting back tears. "I've loved you forever. I tried to blame you when I got pregnant. I tried to hate you because you pursued your dreams. But I know how important dreams are." She took a deep breath. "You went after your dream and you succeeded. I went after my dream, but I didn't succeed." She stared into the depths of his eyes trying to draw strength from him. "I received a call today from the Chicago Symphony. I have an audition Thursday."

He sat still with a stunned look on his face. Finally he broke the prolonged silence. "You have an audition? Thursday? As in you're going to Chicago, Thursday?"

"Actually, I'm flying out Wednesday." He stood and walked toward the large oak tree. His silhouette outlined by the golden sunset. A golden god, with black hair and blue eyes. Tall and straight. Desirable and delightful. Gentle and strong. Good and kind. Honest and dependable.

He turned and asked in a soft, little boy voice, "What about us?"

She walked behind him and wrapped her arms around his waist. Leaning into his back, she said, "Last night you sang that you would love me forever and ever. Can you give me a year? If the audition goes well and I sign the contract, it will only be for a year." Tears flowed down her cheeks. "This is hard because I love you sooo much, but I've dreamed of this, worked for this." She buried her face between his shoulders. "You're good enough to achieve your dream. I need to know that I'm good enough, too. Good enough to reach my dream, and good enough for you."

He turned, wrapping his arms around her, hugging her gently. "Katie, you're good enough for me by just being you, without doing anything." His ragged breathing shook her foundation, weakening her determination. He stroked her hair. "I understand about dreams. I don't want to lose you, but I don't want to hold you down." He stepped back, taking her by the shoulders. "I *will* love you forever and ever. No matter how long it takes. I'll be here waiting for you. One year. Two years. Whatever. Hitch your wagon to a star."

She reached up and stroked his face, tracing his lips with her fingers. "I love you always and forever."

"We could still get married. Then when we're together, we could really be together."

She smiled but shook her head. "Don't tempt me. Let's get through this next week." She dropped her hands and took a step back. The golden light from the sunset formed a halo around his dark hair. Why do all pictures portray angels with yellow hair? They wouldn't if the artists ever saw Brooks Travis. "An audition doesn't mean I'll be offered the position."

"They'd be crazy not to give it to you. You're the best fiddle player I've ever heard, and I've heard some of the best."

"Yes, but this is symphony. A violinist is judged differently than a fiddle player. The director told me one piece to play. It's a difficult score. The rest will be impromptu sight reading."

He took her by the hand and led her to the pickup. "I better get you home so you can start practicing."

When they arrived at her parents' house, he asked, "Do you want me to drive you to the airport?"

"I think my dad will be able to drive now that he has his cast off."

He nodded and stared straight ahead. "I'll still come in the mornings to take care of the stock. In the afternoons, we'll be patching and painting the walls, refinishing the floors, getting ready for the cabinets." When they reached the Kane ranch, he turned back toward her. "I'll wait here until you get inside."

She got out of the pickup and walked to the porch. As she turned to wave, he was already pulling away. He didn't look back.

Inside, Austin and his grandfather were playing dominoes. "When you finish that game, kiss your grandma and grandpa goodnight and come to bed."

"What'd you think of the bathrooms?"

She tousled his hair. "They are beautiful."

"At lunch we went to Abuelo and Grandpa Dustin's house and

236

used their computer to order my blue cowboy bedspread and curtains and a shower curtain and stuff for my bathroom."

"That will look great."

"Maybe we can order yours tomorrow."

"We may need to wait on that for a while." Katie went into their room, took out her violin, and tuned the strings. When Austin came in, she read him a *Frog and Toad* book and then a story from his illustrated children's Bible. After he said his prayer, Katie tucked him in. "Sleep tight and have sweet dreams." She carried her violin to the porch and started playing the arrangement for her audition.

Her dad walked out and sat in his rocker. After a few starts and stops, he said, "Those are some sour notes if ever I heard any."

"Thanks for the encouragement, Dad. It means so much." She picked up her music and stormed to the barn. Turning on the lights, she sat on a bale of hay and started again. Sissy whinnied. "I don't need any criticism from you, too." She tried to play but couldn't see the notes through her tears. She walked over and wrapped her arms around Sissy, crying till the stream ran dry. She patted the horse's neck. "How many times have I used your mane to dry my tears? Every time I had a fight with my mom? Or after Brooks left? When I didn't know what to do?"

She returned to her seat on the hay and played the arrangement through several times, each attempt sounding better than the last. She tiptoed into the house, not wanting to wake her parents.

"That last time sounded much better."

Katie squealed and nearly jumped out of her skin at the sound of her dad's voice. "I thought you would have been asleep a long time ago."

"I can't sleep when something's weighing heavy on my heart. I've been sitting here listening to you and praying. I love you, Katie. I don't want you to hate me, and I don't want to lose you again."

She hugged her father. "You won't lose me, and I could never hate you, no matter what." She kissed him goodnight and went to bed. But she couldn't sleep. Warring images marched through her mind. Images of Brooks and Austin and her in *their* house. Her cooking in their bright white and red kitchen. Drinking coffee watching the sunrise on their patio. Images of her in the symphony, dressed in a formal black gown. Taking a bow when the audience gave a standing ovation. Her dad and mother alone, but not on holidays. She would come home for holidays. Yes, home.

Chapter Thirty-five

Katie spent all day Tuesday practicing the violin, packing and unpacking. Austin clammed up like a dead fish as soon as she told him she was flying to Chicago for an audition with the symphony. The only smile she'd seen was when she told him he could stay with his dad while she was gone. Wednesday morning at breakfast, she reminded him to be on his best behavior. He jumped up as soon as he heard his dad's pickup pull into the drive. Katie grabbed him in a bear hug and kissed his cheek. "I will see you Sunday evening." He tried to pull free, but she held him tight and said, "I love you always and forever." She turned loose, and he grabbed his suitcase and ran out the door, without a word, without so much as a backward glance.

She cleared the table, but her mother insisted on doing the breakfast dishes. "You want to practice your piece one more time? It always made my work more enjoyable when I could hear you play."

Before she began playing, Katie closed her eyes and imagined

239

herself sitting on stage, the spotlight on her as she played a solo. She played the entire piece with her eyes closed. When she finished, her dad said, "That's mighty fine playing, Katie, mighty fine." He stood and emptied his coffee cup. "I'll get your bags after I bring the car around."

"I only have one carryon and my violin. I can get them." He grunted a response and walked out.

"Let him get your bags, Katie. He needs to feel like a man again after being an invalid the past few weeks."

On the drive to Lubbock, her dad played classic country CD's—Sonny James, Johnny Cash, Charlie Pride. When George Jones began singing "The Grand Tour" Katie said, "That has to be one of the most depressing songs ever written. Some guy sitting in the house surrounded by his wife's stuff, having a pity party after she left— pathetic." She shook her head to shake away the image. *Brooks won't be like that if I don't come back, well, especially since none of my stuff will be in his house.* "Don't you ever listen to anything modern?"

"The stuff they play and sing today is not pure country music. Being raised by my grandparents, I cut my teeth on the real deal." He tapped his fingers on the steering wheel. "Life is depressing sometimes. True country music tells about real life. I've known people who never got over their one true love." His eyes met hers in the rearview mirror. "About the only new stuff I listen to is Canada Jones, only because Brooks backed him up."

When "He Stopped Loving Her Today" began playing, Katie said, "You have to admit that song is downright morbid. Can you skip it?"

"Nope. George Jones thought it was morbid, too, the first time he heard it. Bobby Braddock and Curly Putman worked on rewrites for two years before Jones recorded it." He met her eyes in the mirror again. "It's considered the greatest country song of all time. George sang it with passion. He knew what real, true love is. Love that lasts a lifetime."

"It's almost as bad as 'Anna Bell Lee' by Edgar Alan Poe—crazy."

Her mother turned in her seat and said, "That's the poem you memorized in high school for your UIL Oral Reading competition. You went around the house for weeks reciting it, putting so much feeling into it. I was proud when you won a first place ribbon for it. "

"I was a silly, immature drama queen." She stared out the window and watched the West Texas fields fly by, alternating green pastures and barren land burned by the late July heat, the difference between dry land farming and irrigated land. That's how she felt, her emotions fluctuating between the hopeful promise of new life and the downhearted gloom of isolation.

She tuned out the song on the CD player only to have the poem invade her thoughts. *Yes, I was a child and Brooks was a child. We thought our love was more than the love anyone else had ever felt.*

When it ended, I thought my life was over. Did it end? *I thought it did. I thought Brooks stopped loving me.* And did you stop loving him? *"Neither the angels in Heaven above/Nor the demons down under the sea/Can ever dissever my soul from the soul/ Of my beautiful"* . . . Brooks Travis. And the symphony? *Not even the symphony.*

***

Katie's parents walked her to the security checkpoint at the airport. Her dad hugged her and said, "I love you Katie. Knock 'em dead, Sunshine."

"Love you, too, Dad."

Her mother hugged her and said, "I pray that all your dreams will come true. Stay safe. Call when you get to LeAnn's."

"Ok. See you Sunday. Love you."

Her mother squeezed her tight and said, "Love you always and forever."

She walked through the security gate, wondering if she were walking through an open door or slamming one shut behind her.

Chapter Thirty-six

Wednesday Brooks and his grandfathers painted the walls and ceilings while Abuela Carmela and Grandpa Dustin worked in the yard and played with Austin. "This is the whitest house I've ever seen," Gramps said.

"You can put any color with white—it's a blank pallet," Brooks said. "Later on, when I build a master bedroom and bath, I'd like to add on to the front, have a real dining room and larger living room with a vaulted ceiling and wood beams, maybe even a wooden ceiling, and cover the fireplace with rock."

"A master bedroom, huh?" Gramps stepped out on the front porch to put a dip of snuff in his mouth. He hadn't said anything when Brooks told the family that Katie flew to Chicago for an audition, but the foul scowl on his face expressed his displeasure.

Abuelo patted Brooks on the back. "This will be a fine house. It will make a happy home."

243

Brooks nodded and began cleaning up. *Lord, no matter how fine, a house is only a house. It takes love to make a home. I'd love to live here with Katie and Austin, maybe another baby or two, but I want her to be happy. I had my ride. I want Katie to have the same chance to catch her dream. She may be like me and realize that the rainbow she's chasing was right here all along. If not, Lord, you know my heart will be broken, worse than before, because this time I will be giving up the love of my life and my son.*

That night Brooks and Austin had a "sleep over" in the apartment above the barn. They popped popcorn and watched old Disney movies Carmela had saved. Austin said his "Now I lay Me Down to Sleep" prayer and continued, "God, you know I don't want to go back to Chicago and leave my Dad and Poppy and all my grandparents. Please don't let my mom play good. Make her come back and live in our house. Amen."

Okay, Lord, I need some wisdom here. "Austin, do you know how much I love you?"

"Higher than the mountains and deeper than the ocean?"

He brushed the hair off his son's forehead. "Yes, more than words could ever say." He leaned over and kissed Austin on the top of his head. "Well, I love your mom that much, too. And when you love someone, you want them to be happy. This audition is important for her. I pray that she will play better than she's ever played. She's the best violin player I've ever heard. I want her to know that—I want the whole world to know how good she is."

"Don't you want her to live with us in our house?"

"Only if that's what she wants. If she wants to play in the symphony for a year or two, I can wait for her. In the meantime, we can see each other on holidays and school breaks. It will still be our house."

"I want to stay here with you. If Mom plays in the symphony, she'll have to practice all the time. I'll have to stay at the boring afterschool program and then stay in that little apartment the rest of the time. I can't play outside by myself. I can't have Poppy or Mighty Fine. I can't rope or ride horses." He sat up in bed and threw his arms around his dad's neck. "I'll be sad and lonely."

Brooks patted him on the back. "I promise I'll talk to you every day, and we'll see each other a lot." He laid Austin back down and tucked him in. "Go to sleep now, and I'll ask Grandpa Dustin to help you rope tomorrow while I sand the floors. Let's be happy while we're together. Let's just take one day at a time and not worry about what might or might not happen." He kissed him on top of the head and said, "Good night. Sleep tight and have sweet dreams."

"That's what my mom says every night."

"Yes. We used to talk on the phone every night, and we would say it to each other. Even if we don't live in the same house, I can tell you good night every single night."

"I'd rather live with you."

"Good night, Austin."

"Aren't you going to sleep?"

"Not yet, Pardner. I'm going to read my Bible for a while."

Austin patted the bed beside him. "You can lay right here and read your Bible. That's what Mom does. Sometimes she reads it aloud to me."

"She's a good mother." Brooks got undressed and lay down beside his son. Using the app on this phone, he began reading 1 Corinthians 13:3-7 in *The Message*:

"If I give everything I own to the poor and even go to the stake to be burned as a martyr, but I don't love, I've gotten nowhere. So, no matter what I say, what I believe, and what I do, I'm bankrupt without love."

"What's bankrupt mean?"

"It means when you're flat on your face, flat broke."

"Are you flat broke?"

"Not now, but I have been before." *Lord, I don't care about being flat broke, but without Katie I will be flat on my face with no way up.*

"Love never gives up."

"Do you ever give up, Dad?"

"No, my parents and grandfathers taught me to always do my best and to keep on keeping on." *Lord, I don't want to give up on Katie, but I don't know if I can keep on without her and Austin.*

"Love cares more for others than for self."

"Who do you love most?"

"We're supposed to love God more than anything. After that, we're supposed to love our family, husbands and wives, children and parents, grandchildren and grandparents."

"I love you more than my mom."

"Austin, your mother loves you with all her heart. She has always been with you and taken care of you."

"She always tells me I need to share and take turns. Maybe she needs to share and let you have a turn with me."

"Now that I know you, we will share and both of us can take care of you."

"Love doesn't want what it doesn't have."

"Sometimes I want what my friends have that I don't have. I want my mom and dad to
live together like Cantu's parents."

"I want that, too, but we may just have to wait a while before it happens."

"Love doesn't strut,"

"What does strut mean?"

"It means like when someone walks around thinking they're better or more important
than other people."

"Doesn't have a swelled head,"

247

"Have you ever had a swelled head? I had a swelled thumb when I had a splinter in it."

Brooks laughed. "I've had a few knots on my head when I fell off a horse or out of a tree." *And when I got drunk and fell out of my truck. And when I got in a barroom brawl. Don't want to go there again.*

"Doesn't force itself on others, Isn't always 'me first,'"

"Even the Bible says we need to take turns."

Brooks laughed again. "Yes, I guess it does."

"Doesn't fly off the handle,"

"What does that mean?"

"It means don't lose your temper and throw a fit."

"Yeah, if I throw a fit, Mom gives me a time out."

"Austin?"

"Yes, Dad?"

"No matter what happens, if your mom gets the job with the symphony and takes you back to Chicago, try to act like a man. You can scream and cry and throw a fit in front of me, if you need to, but not in front of your mom." Silence. "Will you do that, for me?"

Big sigh. "I'll try."

"Doesn't keep score of the sins of others,"

"What does that mean?"

"It means you don't stay mad. You learn to forgive." *Lord, it took me a long time to forgive myself and Katie. I'm still working on forgiving my dad.*

"Doesn't revel when others grovel,"

"That means don't be glad when other people get in trouble."

"Takes pleasure in the flowering of truth,"

"That means always tell the truth."

"I won't be happy if I have to go back to Chicago. It wouldn't be true if I said I was."

Okay, Lord, give me words of wisdom. "I won't be happy, either, but I will be happy for your mom if she's happy. I'll tell her so. I'll tell her how proud I am of her, that I knew she could do it."

"Puts up with anything,"

"Does that mean like don't hit someone back even if they hit you first?"

"Kind of like that." *Lord, if Katie leaves, that will be a punch in the gut. Please help me support her. Don't let me punch back, no matter what happens.*

"Trusts God always, Always looks for the best, Never looks back, But keeps going to the end."

Brooks turned off his phone and turned off the light. "Good night, Austin. Close your eyes now and go to sleep."

"Good night, Dad."

Lord, I'm trusting in You, to work everything out for our good, for Katie and me, and especially for Austin. I'm looking for the best, which in my mind would be for us to get married and live together as a family, happily ever after. But Your ways and thoughts are higher than ours. I don't want to look back, don't want to go back to the way things were. I want to look forward, to keep my eyes on the prize for which You have called me. I want to serve You with my talents, to be the man You created me to be. I want to be the father and husband You created me to be. Amen.

Chapter Thirty-seven

After dinner, Aunt LeAnn asked Katie to play the arrangement for her audition. LeAnn got her violin and played the same piece. Katie put her head in her hands. "Ugh! You sound so much better than me. I'll never be good enough."

"I am a professional with almost thirty years' experience. This is my life, my entire life." LeAnn showed her where to lengthen the pause, where to pick up the pace. "I'm not hearing your normal passion in this piece. Skill can be developed, but passion is inherent."

"I want to get this position. It's all I've wanted since I was a kid, and I don't want to waste my opportunity."

"If this is what you want, more than anything, then relax. Do your best and leave the rest to God."

Katie closed her eyes, practicing relaxed breathing techniques as she said a silent prayer. She played the piece with all the emotion she could muster.

LeAnn smiled. "Play like that tomorrow, and you will be the next full-time member of the Chicago Symphony." She put away her violin and said, "Give your mind a rest. Let's have a cup of tea and talk about something else." Handing Katie a delicate China cup and saucer with a blueberry scone, she asked, "Your mother and dad are both doing better?"

Katie talked about her dad's walking cast and her mother's improved strength and attitude after finishing chemo. "What have they told you about Brooks?"

"They told me he was back home. He adores Austin." She sipped her tea. "Your mother hinted that he wants a relationship with you, maybe marriage."

Katie took a bite of the scone followed by a sip of tea. "Is that all she said?"

"Pretty much. Just because she and your father have a fairytale happily-ever-after, she thinks everyone can, but unfortunately that's not the case for most people."

"Are you happy? Do you have any regrets?"

"I am happy. I love the symphony." LeAnn walked to the window and stared at the skyline. "There are things about Chicago I love: the symphony, the theatre, the restaurants, the museums. But sometimes I miss home, the wide-open plains of West Texas, the starlit nights, wave after wave in an ocean of blue skies, the lowing of cattle, frogs croaking and crickets chirping, the smell of fresh cut hay and manure." She laughed. "I don't miss the wind, because Chicago is *the* Windy City."

"What about the guy you loved?"

LeAnn sighed. "Donald Howard. He was tall, handsome, and rugged. The son of an oil field worker, destined to life in the oil field, doing dirty, back-breaking work with black fingernails and the constant overpowering smell of oil." She refilled their tea cups. "I wanted culture, refinement, class," she waved her hand across the room, "a penthouse apartment, designer clothes instead of homemade dresses."

LeAnn took a sip of tea. "I got everything I wanted, but I missed out on love." She closed her eyes. "Donald was long and lanky, but muscular and manly. His kiss had the power of a stampeding stallion leading his herd to the precipice. Part of me would have followed him over the cliff, up the mountains, through the valleys. The other part of me wanted more, this *better life*."

"So, do you have any regrets?"

"Yes. Every time I've been interested in a man, I measure them against Donald, and they come up short. Times when I have difficulty sleeping, I wonder what it would be like to be his wife, to have him beside me. I know I wouldn't have been happy being the wife of an oilfield worker." Sadness filled her features. "He worked in the oil fields to pay his way through college. Last I heard, he lived in Houston, an executive for a big oil company." She forced a smile.

"Houston has a symphony. Maybe if I'd been patient, I could have had it all."

"So are you telling me I should take Brooks now and the symphony might work into my future?"

"I would never try to tell you what to do. Your dad and our grandparents, who were the only parents we knew, tried to tell me what to do. I thought they just wanted to keep me down on the farm, out of the big city. My stubborn, rebellious spirit helped make the decision. I've regretted it many times." She shrugged. "If I had married Donald, I would have probably had regrets also." She laughed. "Or maybe I would have had great sex and a house full of kids."

"Aunt LeAnn!"

"I'm 50, not dead."

***

Lying in bed, Katie thought about how it would feel to have Brooks beside her, to cuddle and kiss goodnight. She knew about sleepless nights, alone with no one to cling to, no one to talk to, no one to love. But she did love Brooks. She had never stopped loving him. Or needing him. Or wanting him. Trust was what she lost six years ago, trust in herself as much as in him. Could she trust herself to make the right decision now? Could she trust him? Could they have the fairytale happily-ever-after?

Dear Lord, please help me make the right decision. I want to do well tomorrow and get the position. If I choose to stay in Texas with

Brooks, I don't want him to think it was by default. I want to have a choice, so I can make the right choice.

"But seek first the kingdom of God and His righteousness, and all these things will be added unto you."

Dear Lord, I want to do Your will, but I don't even know what I want, much less what You want.

"Therefore do not worry about tomorrow, for tomorrow will worry about itself. Each day has enough trouble of its own."

I want to trust you with tomorrow and all my tomorrows, but I'm afraid.

"For God has not given us the spirit of fear; but of power, and of love, and of a sound mind."

But how will I know what is right?

"Trust in the LORD with all your heart And do not lean on your own understanding. In all your ways acknowledge Him, And He will make your paths straight."

I do believe You, Lord. Please help my lack of trust and direct my path.

***

Thursday morning, Katie took the transit train and walked to 220 South Michigan Avenue. She stood in awe looking at the 1904 brown brick Symphony Hall, a National Historic Landmark, ringing with over a hundred years of music. The names Bach, Mozart, Beethoven, Schubert, and Wagner inscribed above the ballroom windows on the façade testified of the greatness within. Opening the doors of the huge auditorium, the cold air sucked her breath into the vast expanse. As she walked down the red-carpeted aisle, she imagined moving in slow motion down a church aisle, dressed in a long white gown, in sync with the wedding march, Brooks waiting at the front. Only a few lights illuminated the stage, shrouding the gilded, domed ceiling in shadows. Instead of tall handsome Brooks, Geoffrey Goodwin, III stood—a short, middle-aged man with a slight build and beady eyes. His smile made her think of a copperhead.

Dear Lord, I'm trusting you with today and all my tomorrows. I'm depending on you to help me do my best, to guide my fingers.

Katie prayed the Twenty-third Psalm as she climbed to the stage, each staccato step echoing, "doom-da-doom."

"You look lovely as always, my dear." Goodwin took her hand and kissed it, seemingly sophisticated and smooth, so worldly wise. His long nose reminded her of a goose.

"Thank you, Mr. Goodwin. I appreciate the opportunity to audition with you."

"Please, call me Geoffrey." He kissed her hand again. "I have watched your progress each time you played for the Civic Orchestra and the Symphony. You have an amazing, natural talent like your aunt."

Katie forced a smile. "Thank you. Where would you like me to sit?" He sat in a seat in the front row and patted the seat next to him.

She laid her violin case in that seat and sat in the next one leaving a comfortable space between them.

"Would it help you relax if we talked first, got to know each other better?"

Gazing over the vast auditorium, the seats became a sea of red. Looking up to the second and third-story balconies and the terrace behind the stage, she imagined playing for a full house. Taking a deep breath she said, "I would prefer to play first. We'll have plenty of time to talk later if you decide to offer me the position."

He moved a music stand in front of her. She scooted it back. "I have the piece memorized." She closed her eyes, said a silent prayer, and began to play.

"Bravo!" He clapped his hands. "Perfect!" He opened a briefcase and pulled out some sheet music. "Let's test your impromptu sight reading."

After a few pieces, Goodwin smiled. "You are very good. Let me hear your favorite piece from memory."

Katie played "Amazing Grace" with a heart of gratitude to God for His goodness and grace.

"That is beautiful, but simple. Can you play something more challenging?"

She took a deep breath and began to play Handel's "Arrival of the Queen of Sheba" with her eyes closed.

"Wonderful, lively tempo, and from memory." His animated

257

smile made him look like a cartoon character.

"I played it for my senior recital. I practiced it so much I will never forget it."

He put his hand on her knee. "I would like to take you to dinner to discuss the details of your contract."

"My contract? You're offering me the position?" She jumped up knocking the music stand over. She bent to pick it up the same time he did, and they bumped heads. She could feel the blush creep up her face like a West Texas sunset. "I'm sorry." Avoiding his eyes, she began putting her violin in its case.

"Don't be sorry. I'm glad you're excited about the position."

She stood with her violin case between them. "Thank you. I am overjoyed. But I can't go to dinner with you tonight. Aunt LeAnn made dinner reservations and is taking me to the theatre."

"How about tomorrow night?"

She took a step back and forced a smile. "Could you fax the contract to Aunt LeAnn so I'll have time to look it over before tomorrow?"

"I can fax you a copy. Tomorrow we can discuss any questions you have over dinner. The official contract will need to be signed in person."

She took a card out of her purse. "Here's Aunt LeAnn's fax number. Could you call me tomorrow about where to meet for dinner?"

"I will pick you up at your aunt's apartment at 7:00."

"You know where she lives?"

"I make it a point to know where all my musicians live. Welcome to the family." He tried to hug her, but she kept her violin between them.

Stepping back she said, "Thank you so much. You have made me very happy."

***

When she returned to her aunt's apartment, LeAnn handed her the contract. "Congratulations, Katie. I knew you could do it."

Katie's mouth fell open. "He sent it? He really sent it!" She hugged her aunt. "Have you looked at it? Does it look legit?"

LeAnn laughed. "Yes, I read every word. It is legitimate, but it won't be final until it's signed, in person." She turned Katie toward the guest room. "Go get changed, so we can celebrate."

Katie closed the bedroom door, sat on the bed, and called Brooks. "Hey, whatcha' doin'?"

"I'm working on the floors."

"So how's it coming?"

"I'm almost finished sanding."

"Can you talk? I mean are you alone?"

"Hold on." She could hear heavy boots stomping across the wooden floor, a door closing. "Okay. I'm in the bathroom."

"I just got back from my audition."

He paused before answering, "How'd it go?"

"I got the position. I'm holding the contract in my hand." No response. "Brooks?"

He cleared his throat. "I'm proud of you, Katie. I knew you could do it."

"Brooks?"

She could hear his deep breathing. "Yes?"

"Do you still want to get married?" Her heart skipped a beat.

"You think a long-distance marriage will work?"

"Do you still want to get married?"

"I love you Katie," his hoarse voice wavered. "We'll make it work, somehow."

She flopped backward on the bed and laughed. "Can you come get me?"

"I thought you were flying back Sunday."

"If you can come get me, I can bring my things home, the things I want like the rocker Aunt LeAnn bought me, some kitchen items, our clothes, scrapbooks, books, and Austin's toys. It will give Austin a chance to say goodbye to his friends."

"What are you saying?"

She laughed again. "I'm saying I want to come home, to our home, forever and ever. I want to marry you and live happily ever after. I want the fairy tale." She waited for a response. Thinking he had changed his mind, her heart did a belly flop. "I love you Brooks. Do you still want me?"

"Of course I want you," he said in a breathy voice. "I've always wanted you. I will always want you." He cleared his throat. "I can't promise you a fairy tale, but I'll do my best to make you happy.'

She hugged the pillow and let out a sigh of relief. "How can it not be a fairy tale when you're my handsome Prince Charming? My rainbow is a complete circle. The pot of gold at the end is in Texas where it began." She laughed again and whispered. "I want to get married right away. I want to begin our happily ever after as soon as possible. I want a whole tribe of Travises to fill up our house."

"Do you want to get married in Chicago?"

Giggling she said, "No, silly. I don't want a big fancy wedding, but I do want our family to be there."

"I'll call the band leader and tell him I can't play Sunday. Then I'll take a shower and Austin and I will hit the road."

"Don't drive all night. I want to see you tomorrow. And every day for the rest of my life. You make my heart sing."

"You have just made me the happiest man in the world. I love you so much."

The fervor spread from her face to her toes. "I love you more."

"No, I love you more." He laughed. "I'll call and let you know when we stop."

"Aunt LeAnn is taking me out to our favorite little Italian Restaurant and to the theater to see *Beauty and the Beast*. If my phone is off, leave a message and I'll call you back when I get home."

"Are you calling your parents, or do you want me to?"

She sighed. "Would you think it was too hokey and old fashioned if I wanted you to talk to my parents and ask for their blessing?"

"Anything for you, Katie. Talk to you later. I love you." He put his hand over his racing heart as in a pledge.

"I love you, too."

Chapter Thirty-eight

Brooks pumped his fist in the air. *Yes! Thank You, Lord.*

He boot-scooted it out of the bathroom. His dad and grandfathers stared at him in wonder as he took off his tool belt. "We're calling it a day. I'm going to get Katie."

"Was she disappointed she didn't get the job?" Abuelo asked.

Brooks felt the grin spread across his face. "Nope, cause she got it."

"So why are you going to get her?" His dad asked with a scowl.

"Because she's coming home. To our home. We're getting married."

"How you think that will work with her in Chicago and you here?" Gramps asked, stretching his back.

"She got the position, but she turned it down so we can get married and live happily ever after." He patted Gramps on the shoulder.

"Happily ever after, huh?" his dad asked.

"That's our plan."

Abuelo hugged his grandson. "It's a very good plan."

"While you're gone, we'll finish the floors so they'll be ready for the cabinets," Gramps said, putting a dip of snuff in his mouth.

"You getting married in Chicago?" his dad asked.

"Nope. We want the whole family to be there, if Celina can come home."

"Better tell your mom the date so she can start making plans." His dad looked at the other men. "Let's get back to work."

***

Brooks had to fight his led foot on the drive to the T-C Quarter Horse Ranch. He didn't want to deal with a ticket. When he entered the house, Austin was helping Abuela make flour tortillas. Brooks tousled Austin's black hair. Hugging his mother, he asked, "How long until dinner?"

"An hour or so. Did you all quit working early today?"

"Just me. I'm going to take a shower and pack some clothes, so Austin and I can go get Katie."

"I didn't think my mom was coming back till Sunday."

Brooks picked Austin up and swung him around. "There's been a change in plan. We're going to get her so we can bring your stuff here to our house and let you say goodbye to your friends."

Austin threw his arms around his dad's neck. "Yay, she didn't get the job!"

Brooks held him at arm's length. "Yes, she did get the job because she's the best fiddle player ever." Austin's lip quivered. Brooks lifted his chin, looked him in the eyes, and said, "But she turned it down. She chose us. We're getting married."

Austin's face lit up. "When are we getting married?"

"Soon. Very soon. Help Abuela Carmela finish the tortillas so we can eat something before we hit the road." He hugged his mother. "After dinner can you call Celina and see if she can get a flight home? We can call Andrea when a definite date is set."

Carmela wiped tears from her eyes. "I am so happy for you. I pray you will have a beautiful life."

"Keep praying, and we'll give it our best shot."

***

After eating a quick supper with the family, Brooks tossed his duffle bag and Austin's suitcase in the back of the pickup. "We'll stop by to talk to the Kanes and get Austin some more clothes. I'll call you tonight and let you know where we stop and again tomorrow when we get there."

"Be careful where you stop. Some places aren't safe." Dustin took out his money clip and offered Brooks a wad of bills.

"Thanks, Dad, but I've got some cash, a debit card, and a credit card."

"Take it. I haven't done anything for you since you left home."

Brooks hugged his father. "You always provided for the family and you've done a lot helping with my house." He patted his father on the back. "Save it, and if you want, you can give it to us as a wedding gift." When he stepped back, he saw tears in his father's eyes. He hugged him again. "I love you, Dad." He kissed his mother and hugged each of his grandfathers before leading Austin out to the pickup.

When they pulled onto Kane Lane, Brooks said, "Let me tell them the good news, okay?" Austin nodded in response.

"We didn't expect to see you until Sunday morning." Donna looked worried. "Is everything alright?"

Brooks twisted his hat in his hands. "We need to get Austin another change of clothes or two." He couldn't keep the smile from spreading across his face. "We're driving to Chicago to get Katie and some of their stuff."

Donna shook her head. "I hope she's not too disappointed she didn't get the job."

"She . . ." Austin stopped when his dad gave him a stern look.

"She did get the position, but she decided not to take it."
Brooks cleared his throat. "I would like to ask your permission to
marry Katie. We want to get married . . . soon."

Donna squealed, hopped up, and hugged him. "I'm so happy.
You don't need our permission, but we give you our blessing."
Turning toward her husband she asked, "Don't we?"

Richard wiped a hand over his eyes. "You know, Katie is high
strung and strong willed. She's not easy to get along with, but she'll
always be our little girl. We give you our blessing if you promise to be
good to her, to love her and be faithful, no matter what, 'til death do
you part."

Brooks stepped in front of Richard's chair and extended his
hand. "I do." He laughed. "I mean I promise."

"Are you getting married in Chicago?" Donna asked.

"No ma'am. We don't want a big fancy wedding, but we want
all of our family to be with us."

"Austin, let's go get you some clothes." Donna led the boy to
the bedroom.

Richard said, "Katie is a lot like her mother. Donna hasn't
always been the easiest person to get along with either, but she has
always been a good wife and mother. You've got to learn to pick your
battles. I let her have her way about most things, like the house. We
discuss and try to make decisions together about the important stuff.
I've been the provider, but I haven't always fulfilled my responsibility

as the spiritual leader and head of the house. I pray you'll do a better job than me."

"I think you've done a fine job. I admire and respect you."

Donna and Austin returned with a bulging backpack. "I'll be praying for safe travels. You're not driving all night are you?"

"No, if we can make it to Oklahoma City tonight, we should be able to make it to Chicago tomorrow."

She kissed Austin and hugged Brooks. "Please let us know when you stop and when you get there tomorrow."

Chapter Thirty-nine

Austin pointed at their apartment building. "That's it! The parking garage is in the back. We never parked there because we don't have a car. We take the transit train, sometimes the bus."

Brooks pulled into the parking garage. Katie had called ahead to security, so Austin led the way to the elevator and through the hallway to their apartment. He rang the doorbell and said, "Lift me up so Mom can see me through the peep hole." They heard Katie unlock and unlatch several locks and chains. When she opened the door, she stepped into Brooks's open arms. Austin threw his arms around both parents and said, "Group hug!"

Once inside, Katie closed the door and secured the locks and chains. Brooks raised his eyebrows. "Better safe than sorry," she said. "I've gone through the kitchen and have packed what I want to take. The only furniture I want is my rocking chair, the dressing table in my bedroom, the bookcase, and Austin's toy box. The rest we can donate to Goodwill, unless you think we might need anything for our house."

"Whatever you want. The cabinets and kitchen will be done this week. That should give us enough time to get furniture before the wedding."

"I've been on the phone with our moms all day. Celina and Andrea can be here in two weeks, and of course Aunt LeAnn will book her flight as soon as we set the definite date. Will that be too soon for you? To get married, I mean?"

"Not soon enough." He took her in his arms and kissed her.

***

Sunday morning they met Aunt LeAnn for brunch. She smiled at Brooks. "Katie made the right choice. Nothing in Chicago looks as good as you."

"Aunt LeAnn! I'm shocked."

She laughed. "I told you I'm 50, not dead."

Cantu's family picked Austin up at the train station so the boys could have a play date.

Aunt LeAnn gave Brooks a tour of Symphony Hall. "I've played in some big places, but nothing as fancy as this," he said.

Katie looked around. "It takes my breath away."

Brooks raised his eyebrows. "Are you having second thoughts?"

She threw her arms around his neck and whispered in his ear, "You do more than take my breath away." And she kissed him.

LeAnn cleared her throat. "Umm, you're not alone here. And the wedding is not for what, two weeks?"

Katie dropped her arms and stepped back. "You're right. I need to finish packing and clean the apartment so the superintendent can inspect it."

"Can I do anything to help?"

Katie hugged her aunt. "You have done more than enough the past six years, well, even before that—helping me get my scholarship."

"You earned that scholarship, and I enjoyed having family close by after all those years living alone."

"We'll come see you at least once a year." Katie looked at Brooks pleadingly. "Can't we, I mean to go to the symphony and the theatre?"

"Sure." He smiled at LeAnn. "And you can come to see us anytime. How long's it been since you've been to Texas?"

"I haven't been there since Katie graduated from high school, but that's going to change, starting in two weeks." LeAnn handed Brooks an envelope. "I don't know if you'll have time to register, so I'm giving you this now. I want you to get some nice dishes as a wedding gift. I usually get Waterford Crystal, but I don't think that's your style."

They parted at the Transit station. Katie and Brooks loaded his truck, and they picked up Austin at Cantu's house. As they reached the highway, Katie said, "Today is the first day of the rest of our life."

Brooks patted her knee and smiled. "Goodbye, Chicago. Hello, Texas."

Bonus Chapter

If you would like to read a bonus chapter of *Somebody Somewhere in Texas,* the beginning beyond the end, where Katie and Brooks finish their house, get married, and begin a new life of happily ever after, send me an email, and I will send it to you, complete with pictures.

The next book will be Andrea's love story. After graduating from veterinarian college, she will meet a hunky, manly man who will "light up her life." Watch for details on my website: http://connielewisleonard.webs.com/

Facebook: Connie Lewis Leonard, Author.

Email (if you want to receive the bonus chapter): rycon70@att.net

From the Author:

Connie Lewis Leonard

"I can do all things through Christ who strengthens me." Philippians 4:13

Redeemed, how I love to proclaim it! Christ called me to salvation when I was eleven. At seventeen, I married the love of my life. We have been married for more than forty-six years and have been blessed with two children and three grandchildren. After working to put my husband through college and seminary, God gifted me with academic scholarships for college and graduate school. I was a member of Sigma Tau Delta National English Honor Society and was inducted into *Who's Who in American Colleges and Universities*. I have a BS in education and a MA in English, with a published thesis titled *Mark Twain: The Voice of Innocence and Innocence Corrupted.* For twenty-three years I taught English and English/language arts in public schools, followed by two years teaching in a private homeschool co-op. Now I am pursuing my life-long dream of writing.

I am a member of American Christian Fiction Writers, ACFW/DFW Ready Writers, North Texas Christian Writers, and

Granbury Writers' Bloc. In order to learn the business of writing and further develop my skills, I have attended numerous local, regional, and national conferences and workshops, including Romance Writers of America, ACFW, CLASSeminars, NTCW Mentoring Clinic, and Christian Writers Guild Craftsman Course. I have published devotions in *Out of the Overflow* (WinePress Publishing, 2011) and *Transformed* (WinePress Publishing, 2012). Several of my short stories and devotions have been published in area anthologies, and over fifty articles have been published in regional magazines. I have written and taught ladies' Bible studies "Praying the Lord's Prayer" and "Hearing the Voice of God." I enjoy speaking at ladies' retreats and conferences. My novel, *Big C, little c,* was published in 2014. My interactive devotional Bible study, *A Psalm a Day,* was published in 2015. They are available through Amazon in paperback and Kindle.

Visit my website: http://connielewisleonard.webs.com/

Visit me on Facebook: Connie Lewis Leonard, Author

Big C, little c

By Connie Lewis Leonard

Lyn Newton's foundation is rocked by the diagnosis of cancer. Assaulted by one crisis after another, her family fights for life, life as they've known it, life as they hope it will be, and finally the life Christ has planned for them. With prayer and the support of Lyn's ladies' Bible study group, they discover the peace of Christ, "The Big C," who is greater than any calamity of life, including cancer. Through laughter and tears, the Newton family is drawn back together, stronger in love for each other and faith in God.

"Connie Leonard writes with passion, empathy, and understanding because she has personally faced a battle with cancer and survived. Her storytelling reflects the frustration, determination, and endurance needed to cope with the emotional and physical challenges of a disease. This is a page-turning book."

Dr. Dennis E. Hensley
author, *Jesus in the 9 to 5*

"Connie Leonard's struggle and victory over cancer comes alive in *Big C Little c.* She has masterfully crafted a novel about a woman who courageously fought the same battle with cancer and relied on God for healing strength. I recommend this novel to any woman who has ever loved a cancer victim."

DiAnn Mills
FIREWALL, Tyndale,
July 2014

Available at amazon.combooks in paperback and Kindle version.

A Psalm a Day

By Connie Lewis Leonard

A Psalm a Day is an interactive devotional Bible study. Each daily devotion focuses on a specific Psalm. The Bible study cross references other verses, using multiple translations of the Bible. Since God speaks to His children through music, and the book of Psalms is poetry often set to music, many Christian songs are included to enrich the connections between the Psalms and our daily life. The author includes personal accounts of how the Psalms have impacted her.

The book of Psalms addresses every human emotion. A Psalm a Day interactive devotional Bible study is written to encourage readers through the valleys and inspire you on the mountain tops. May this book help you transform your Fear into Faith, Pain into Praise, Worries into Worship, Tests into Testimonies, Defeats into Victories, and Battles into Blessings.

Available at amazon.combooks in paperback and Kindle version.

Made in the USA
San Bernardino, CA
16 March 2017